10 Things Aliens Hate About You

Alienn, Arkansas 4

FIONA ROARKE

10 THINGS ALIENS HATE ABOUT YOU
ALIENN, ARKANSAS 4
Copyright © 2019 Fiona Roarke

ISBN: 978-1-944312-24-4

Want to know when Fiona's next book will be available?
Sign up for her Newsletter: http://eepurl.com/bONukX

To my devoted readers who have waited
so long for this book, thank you for loving my
alien world hiding in plain sight in Arkansas.

Available Now from Fiona Roarke

BAD BOYS IN BIG TROUBLE

Biker
Bouncer
Bodyguard
Bomb Tech
Bounty Hunter
Bandit

Coming soon
Billionaire

NOCTURNE FALLS UNIVERSE COLLECTION

Aliens Actually
Close Encounters of the Alien Kind
Invasion of the Alien Snatchers
The Alien Who Fell to Earth

Merry & Bright: A Christmas Anthology
Have Yourself a Merry Little Alien

The Dragon's Spellbound Alien
The Vampire's Unintended Alien
The Witch's Enchanted Alien

Winter Wonderland: A Christmas Quartet
Baby, It's Alien Outside

Valvoline Ethyl Grey, the youngest sibling and only daughter in the Grey clan, knows the rules when it comes to Alpha-human relationships—it's fine to have a little fun, just don't get too attached, unless you want a one-way ticket back to a homeworld that's never been home.

Skeeter Bite Sheriff Wyatt Campbell is as easygoing as they come, but even he has his limits. At first he thought Vee wanted to keep their romance under wraps to protect him from a butt-kicking from one—or all—of her six brawny older brothers. Since they seem to like him well enough, that can hardly be the case. Now he just has to convince his commitment-shy girlfriend to take a chance. She already has his heart. Why not his ring?

A woman raised among oblivious humans in a super-secret alien colony in Alienn, Arkansas should know better than to have a super-secret love affair with a human, let alone a sheriff. But strong-willed Valene is all too weak when it comes to a certain tall, blond and utterly scrumptious lawman.

Although he comes to her family's aid when they need him most and vows to keep the secret from other humans that aliens live among them, Valene is determined to sacrifice her love for Wyatt's greater good.

Wyatt has other plans.

Chapter 1

Valene Grey, along with the rest of the assembled chili cook-off crowd, waited with barely contained anticipation to hear the judge declare the big winner.

"And the winner of the blue ribbon—and bragging rights—for the best chili creation this year is...Southern Fried Chili from Skeeter Bite's very own Critters Café, and owner and operator Daphne Charlene Dumont." The judge clapped heartily along with a smattering of applause from the other judges and the crowd, most of it from the Critters Café staff over by their chili stand.

Daphne Charlene squealed with joy and raced up the handful of stairs to join the judges. "Thank you all so much! I'm honored, of course, since this is my first time even entering a contest."

She accepted the blue ribbon and a sizeable winnings envelope with another squeal, waiting with a huge grin on her face for the photographer to get a shot of her with the judges and her prize. While she seemed sincere, her acceptance speech did not go over well with the other contestants.

A hush fell over the crowd…for about three seconds after her exuberant acceptance speech. The flash of the local newspaper's photographer taking the picture seemed to light up the crowd. Until then, Valene thought they all looked like they were in shock over the stunning announcement. One camera flash and their true feelings came out with a vengeance.

"There is no way that slop is the best chili this year," came a cranky yet familiar voice from the center of the assembled group. *Do I know that voice?* Valene Grey contemplated who it could be, or rather, who it probably *was*, but didn't have time to fully evaluate that notion before the restless mob of participants and chili lovers devolved into an accusatory shouting match.

The lead judge frowned. "It *is* the best one. All five of us judges agreed. It was unanimous." Behind him, looking nervous, the other four judges nodded in agreement, their eyes on the audience with clearly growing concern.

"No! You're dead wrong! My creation is the best one," shouted a nearby participant. "I've never lost with my secret recipe."

"You're crazy. I should be the winner. My chili is best!" screamed another angry chili contestant, flinging a filled sample bowl at the first guy.

A gloppy spatter of Hoe Down's Best Hot Chili sprayed the front of Valene's pink T-shirt en route to its intended target, the owner of Chuckle Charlie's Chili Shed. Looking down at the mess dripping down her chest and already soaking though to the skin in several places, Valene knew her favorite top was about to become a rag-bag candidate.

Chili stains were forever.

Valene looked up just in time to duck as Chuckle Charlie himself hurled a bowl of chili that arced through the air toward the initiator of the battle. Valene shot a glance behind her, and watched as another innocent victim of the now crazed chili vendetta—an older gentlemen wearing thick glasses—was splattered in the face. He took his glasses off, revealing blinking eyes and the wrinkled bridge of his nose as the only parts of his face not covered in sauce. A large glob of chili slid from his forehead down his nose.

Aunt Dixie—right in the middle of the pandemonium, because where else would she be—tried to help calm the savage crowd, but her quiet voice went unheard in the general melee. Her ever-present partner in crime and helper, Miss Penny, also tried to soothe the mob. That lasted for all of two seconds before the elderly ladies exchanged knowing smiles and joined the fray, chucking tasting cup after tasting cup of Maxwell the Martian's Favorite Chili at the combatants.

It was a sad fate for Alienn, Arkansas's signature chili recipe, courtesy of the Cosmos Café, which advertised it as, "Chili worth traveling the cosmos for a single taste." The tagline was even emblazoned on the menu board above the café's pass-through window to the kitchen.

Valene could only stare in disbelief. Sure, the rivalries inspired by the annual chili contest were legendary, and the competitors could be downright scary. But this was something else. The contestants seemed more unhappy than usual with the judges' choice of blue-ribbon winner.

Was it because Daphne Charlene was young? Really pretty? Any man's dream come true? Perhaps those factors contributed to the sour grapes on such flagrant display, but more than likely it was because it was the new business owner's first time entering a contest up against a wide field of cooks who were more seasoned in local contest circles. Perhaps having a newbie come in and steal the show was a pill too bitter to swallow. Whatever the reason, the discussion wouldn't be settled by hurling bowls of chili at one another.

Daphne Charlene Dumont, first-time chili cook-off contestant, had won over the judges with her southern-fried chili bowl fair and square, Valene figured. Basically, she took small pieces of pork and beef deep-fried in a corn bread batter and added them to her chili, putting extra pieces on top for garnish. Valene had tried a blind taste test sample earlier and thought it was delicious, but she didn't dare admit that to any of the incensed contest losers.

Daphne Charlene's chili caused an uproar almost the instant the scent of hot peppers and savory meat hit the air. All twenty-nine of her opponents cried foul over Daphne Charlene's methods, saying that adding fried corn bread was cheating. The lead judge disagreed. "I'm the deciding judge here and I not only choose the winner, I choose the contestants."

He was trying to repeat his bold statement now, shouting as best he could to be heard over the din as kidney beans and scarlet sauce flew through the air in a display more gruesome than any war zone. "This chili is the best one for this year's contest. And if you don't like it, too bad! My judgment is final."

"Food fight!" shrieked the familiar voice in the crowd and things went from bad to worse. Valene had a moment to be thankful there were only thirty booths set up for the event. The sponsors had put a cap on the number of participants due to the space available for public parking. Otherwise, there would be quite a few more than thirty booths to snatch tasty chili missiles from. Well, twenty-nine booths.

A battalion's worth of projectiles in the form of bowls, cups and other containers of chili went airborne for another volley into the scattering crowd.

Anarchy ruled.

Valene stared at the senseless chili warfare display and wondered how she got here. It wasn't like she hadn't sort of expected things to erupt into chaos. Admittedly, she hadn't expected a chili bowl food fight, but bad luck and trouble often seemed to follow her these days.

That didn't used to be true. She'd had regular, average luck her whole life. Lately, not so much.

Perhaps her new sister-in-law's parents had put an Alpha alien curse on her because of what had happened at Axel's wedding several months back. Even though Axel and his new wife were completely delighted. What else could Valene have done? It wasn't like she could stand by while her brother was forced to marry the sister of the woman he loved. Axel and Lucy were much more suited to each other, and Francine insisted she was better off, too, though she'd paid a very high price for refusing to marry Axel. Axel's in-laws eventually warmed to the idea, somewhat—because they basically had to—but seeing as how Valene had been instrumental in how things had turned out during that whole wedding affair, it was feasible someone in the universe wasn't very happy with her.

She had no regrets.

A column of warm chili slammed into her

shoulder and dripped down her arm, pulling her out of her stroll down memory lane and into the present. She shook most of it off, took a deep breath, walked boldly into the middle of the chaos and roared, "Enough! Stop throwing chili right now, this second!"

The mob froze in shocked silence. Then, everyone around her lowered the bowls, cups and various containers, but didn't discard them.

"Do you all want to go to jail? This is a public park, for Pete's sake, not a fraternity house. Stop all of this craziness before someone calls the sheriff."

As if she'd arranged for it in advance, the thin wail of a siren rose in the distance. It was getting louder. Valene looked toward the skies, issuing a silent plea it wasn't the sheriff. She'd cheerfully face down a deputy or a rent-a-cop or absolutely anyone other than Skeeter Bite's chief lawman.

Someone in the crowd yelled, "It's the cops! I'm outta here!"

Like juvenile delinquents caught standing with dripping cans of spray paint in front of a defaced wall, all around Valene folks dropped the chili bowls, cups and other containers to the ground and raced to their booths. They threw utensils, pots and leftover ingredients into the backs of the pickup trucks, SUVs and trailers that had brought them to the cook-off and made their getaways. In less than two shakes of a lamb's tail, the better part of the chili-making crowd was racing away, honking at others doing the same thing and exiting the park with as much order as a demolition derby.

That left Valene, Aunt Dixie and Miss Penny to face law enforcement with the few remaining chili-splattered attendees.

Naturally, it had to be the sheriff of Skeeter Bite. Wyatt Campbell.

Wyatt drove in one side of the parking area as the contestants' vehicles streamed out the opposite end. He turned off his siren, parked and got out of his official vehicle, scowling as road dust swirled in the air around him. He approached the hot zone.

Wyatt glanced around at the remaining bystanders, took in their chili-stained clothing and rueful expressions. Daphne Charlene looked bewildered. The five judges cowered on the makeshift stage. Valene, Aunt Dixie and Miss Penny stood with several other seemingly stunned folks caught in the crossfire while attending what the uninitiated might expect to be a wholesome, family-friendly public event.

"What in tarnation happened here?" he asked. His semi-choked tone told Valene he was probably doing his best to keep a big grin from coming to rest on his gorgeous lips.

She forced herself to meet his eyes. He had no idea she'd about come to the conclusion she'd have to break up with him. Not that anyone but the two of them would know, since she'd worked very hard to keep things on the down low. It was coming time to end their secret relationship. Their sweet, sexy, steaming hot secret relationship.

She was stuck. Although she'd been wracking her brains for months, she hadn't figured out a way to sidestep the weighty—and completely unfair—rules set by Alpha-Prime or the ones enforced by her own family. Simply put, a permanent bond with Wyatt, a human, was a one-way ticket off Earth. If she couldn't find a way, and soon, she'd have to give him up. Her heart seized for a beat at the coming loss.

She loved Wyatt. She loved her family. It was an impossible situation, being forced to choose between leaving Earth with the love of her life and staying with her family on the only world she'd ever known. While she hadn't given up, she was close to being forced to make that very horrible decision.

Wyatt, of course, had no idea his girlfriend was an alien from Alpha-Prime.

Daphne Charlene, who watched Wyatt avidly as soon as his cruiser pulled in, suddenly raced down the steps of the gazebo to fling herself against his chest, wrapping her arms around his neck. She sobbed out a few words, then stopped trying to talk and just cried on him.

He didn't touch her, at least not at first. Finally, he patted her back awkwardly with one palm, his gaze on Valene.

She returned his stare, knowing hers held a

longing component because she was in love with him. She kept herself in check as best she could, resisting the urge to tear the other woman away from him. They were in public, and she couldn't do anything that might give away the fact they were a couple. An on-again, off-again couple. More on than off because Valene was weak. Every time she tried to leave him or say they needed some space, she was unable to stay away from him. Valene was in love with a human and his name was Sheriff Wyatt Campbell, the operative word being *human*.

If she continued a romantic relationship with him and they got married, he would have to be told about the aliens that were living in Alienn, Arkansas. Her whole family had come to Earth from another planet a few generations before with the human population none the wiser. Humans on Earth were *never* to know about them or where they came from. No exceptions. None.

First, Wyatt would need to be told about aliens living in plain sight in Alienn, running a huge galactic way station under the Big Bang Truck Stop. Then, he'd have to agree to move with Valene to her home planet of Alpha-Prime. If he didn't agree, he'd be given a massive dose of drugs to make him forget all he'd learned about them, and her. He'd be released to live his human life, without her or any memory of their relationship.

It was vastly unfair. Valene wanted Wyatt with every breath she took. She hated to see him with a beautiful girl hugged up against him. She had to bite her tongue and think happy thoughts to keep from lowering her head, kicking one foot through the chili laden grass a few times before charging forward to butt the two of them apart, arena-bull style.

Wasn't it bad enough she was named after motor oil and old gasoline? Did she have to suffer this public humiliation as well? It was a question she asked herself often. Her parents thought her name was beautiful and had no doubts. Valene had plenty of regrets.

Valvoline Ethyl Grey was the name on her birth certificate. Even with that handicap and the additional curse of six older and extremely protective brothers, she'd still managed to find the perfect man to fall in love with.

A man who loved her despite those two very unfortunate truths. A man who had a special endearment he called her when it was just the two of them alone together. A man she would likely not get to keep forever. Because he didn't know about the most important aspect of her life. She was an alien from another planet. He was a gorgeous earthling and never the twain shall meet.

Even though she wanted him in the worst way. Even if she were willing to move to a planet two galaxies away—and she wasn't—Wyatt would never go for it. He was part of a large, close-knit family. He'd have to leave the planet without a trace and no one in his big family could ever know where he'd gone or why. He'd simply disappear.

A totally unfair scenario.

Sheriff Wyatt Campbell was flawless in every single way, except for the part about being a human. Not that being human was a problem in general, but Valene couldn't marry a human and remain on Earth. She had to choose—leave her family and move to another galaxy or give up Wyatt. Stupid rules. And in Valene's albeit biased judgment, they were really, truly the stupidest rules every conceived by, well, aliens.

Humans were never to know aliens lived in plain sight in Alienn, Arkansas or in the offshoot colony in Nocturne Falls, a small town in Georgia. Never!

Valene had even secretly checked to see if she and Wyatt could move to Georgia and live in peace. Nova, her brother Diesel's office assistant, had helped her send the inquiry to Alpha-Prime's Headquarters of Extra-terrestrial Affairs. HETA replied unequivocally a week ago: Denied, never, big-fat-no, don't even think about it.

Valene was out of ideas. For now.

But how long would Wyatt wait? He'd been pretty patient with what he assumed to be a commitment-phobic girlfriend, but she knew he wanted to marry her. He'd even spoken to her eldest brother about dating her, since their parents were out of town more often than not in recent years. Wyatt thought he was talking to the de facto head of her family, when really he was addressing the Arkansas colony's Fearless Leader.

Diesel told Valene that while he liked Wyatt, no exception to the rules would be made if they married. He left it to her to determine what to do next. But that was the problem. Valene didn't know what to do.

Given the extent of Wyatt's family in Arkansas, it would be a very difficult choice for him to leave. Even if he were willing to move off-world, he'd likely balk at the prospect of leaving them to mourn his mysterious disappearance forever.

Wyatt was second eldest of five children and the only boy. She didn't want to move away from her family, either, but at least they'd know where she was and could visit her on occasion.

She and Wyatt both understood big, loud families. It was one of the many things they had in common. Her favorite thing they had in common was kissing. She wanted to kiss him now. The visual of ramming Daphne Charlene out of the way so Valene could kiss his perfect mouth circled in her mind once more.

The only workaround she'd thought of was moving in with him and living in what some humans called sin. What could anyone on Alpha-Prime do if she didn't officially marry her human? She didn't know, and until she understood the potential fallout of such a bold, unconventional move, she didn't want to do anything that might jeopardize any possible future with Wyatt.

Daphne Charlene finally released Wyatt. He moved away with a distracted pat on her shoulder, and walked straight to Valene.

"Would you care to explain what happened here?"

"Nope."

Wyatt's mouth quirked into a quick smile and then it went away. He put a hand on his gun, leaned in close and whispered in her ear, "You have a piece of chili bean on your upper lip and I'd really like to kiss it off. What do you say?"

Chapter 2

Wyatt Campbell likely should not have said what he had to Valene Grey, even though he meant every word. The woman made him crazy in all the best ways, but she was also gun-shy about their relationship and he hadn't been able to figure out why.

"Better not," Valene said in a rush, color coming into her lovely cheeks as she wiped her mouth and mostly brushed away the errant lucky chili bean off her beautiful face. He would have rather kissed it off, but wasn't supposed to acknowledge their feelings in public.

She moved half a step away, perhaps to stay out of range of the kiss he knew they both wanted. He understood. He didn't doubt her love for him, even though he knew she often held herself back. It was as if she feared if she let herself go, she wouldn't be able to retreat to her neutral corner.

Valene did have six older brothers. Wyatt knew them all and they seemed to like him well enough. He'd even spoken to her eldest brother about dating her. When pressed, Diesel told him he didn't have a problem with Wyatt dating his little sister, though he'd have to speak to their father if things got serious. Wyatt understood that, and was ready and willing.

He and Valene were completely serious as far as Wyatt was concerned. The elder Greys were tough ones to pin down, though. First, they'd been rambling around on an RV road trip across the country, return date unknown. Zebulon and Xenia Grey returned briefly to attend the wedding of Valene's brother, Axel, then skedaddled faster than a rocket-propelled rabbit the day after the nuptials.

Wyatt had attended, too, but hadn't been able to sit with Valene, as she was one of the wedding coordinators or something. She sought him out at the extravagant reception for a private dance in the woods, just the two of them, within earshot of the band playing some eighties love song. He didn't care what they played. He enjoyed dancing with the love of his life—correction, the *super-secret* love of his life.

They'd kissed. And kissed. And kissed. Valene pushed him against a tree and kissed him until he wasn't certain he could let her go.

The shout wrenched her out of their passionate and involved embrace.

"Valvoline Ethyl Grey! Where are you?" The female voice called out twice more before Valene broke away, put shaky fingers to her lips and stared at him with wide blue eyes.

"Please don't go, Vee," he'd whispered and reached for her. She shook her head and said softly, "I have to go, Wyatt. I'm so sorry." She scurried away as if fearful of being seen with him.

Story of their relationship. Passionate, crazy, incredible kisses followed by stark and lengthy distances. Valene dictated their together time. Always had and likely always would.

He wanted to put his foot down. He wanted to shout how much he loved her from every rooftop in the nearest three towns. He divided most of his time between Skeeter Bite, Old Coot and Alienn, Arkansas. If he had his way, he would have already put a ring on her finger and married her. They could even have a baby on the way by now, if only she would settle down and let him in.

An elusive something, one he couldn't quite put his finger on, was in the way of their permanent happiness. One day he'd figure out what it was, fix it and move on to enjoy the life with Valene he'd only dreamed of thus far. Until then, he waited with growing exasperation for the love of his life to stop running and let him catch her for good.

There wasn't anything he wouldn't do to make Valene Grey happy. Which he'd told her, repeatedly. She would get a wistful look in her eye and mumble something along the lines of, "I wish that could be true."

Recently, he'd gone to his father, the town's former sheriff, for advice. Before he could say anything about the trouble he was having nailing down a permanent relationship with Valene, his father asked if he was dating anyone special. At first, Wyatt was relieved to have the opening. Clearly his parents had noticed something was off with their son and his mother had delegated his father to suss out whatever it was. His father wondered out loud if his only son ever planned to settle down. Wyatt said there might be someone he was interested in, but he hadn't taken it to the next level yet for a variety of reasons. All of them had to do with Valene and her skittishness. He'd promised Valene he'd be discreet about their relationship, even with his family, so he couldn't bring himself to name her to his father outright.

Wyatt figured his father knew about Valene anyway, and was fishing for confirmation. He hoped maybe the ex-sheriff, who was on good terms with Valene's parents, might speak up to them on Wyatt's behalf. But he'd been wrong.

Shortly after their man-to-man talk, his parents invited Daphne Charlene Dumont to their house for a family dinner and seated her next to Wyatt. The father-son conversation came immediately to Wyatt's mind. Either his father hadn't known about Valene or his parents wanted to dissuade Wyatt from pursuing her by setting him up with a local woman they already approved of.

Wyatt endured a very long dinner with Daphne Charlene and his family, where it was obvious why she was there and everyone, including three out of his four sisters in attendance, gushed over what a great couple they made. It was all Wyatt could do not to roll his eyes at the setup.

Daphne Charlene was an attractive girl. One of the most unappealing things about her was she seemed very aware of that fact. But since Wyatt was generally a positive kind of guy, he allowed she might have many fine qualities that some other man might appreciate. She was accomplished in her career, owning and operating Skeeter Bite's newest and most popular restaurant, Critters Café. That interesting name always made him think of roadkill, but he'd never be so rude as to say that out loud and no one else seemed to feel that way.

Her restaurant was in a grand refurbished historical building on a small hill nestled at the edge of dense woods. The onetime dry goods store supposedly had a speakeasy hidden in the basement during Prohibition. Daphne Charlene had turned the place into a relaxed eating establishment where any and all, from prom attendees dressed to the nines to simple farm folk, could come in and be comfortable.

Wyatt tried to like Daphne Charlene for his parents' sake, but certainly not in a romantic way. Yes, she was beautiful. Yes, she was smart. Yes, she was successful. Yes, he was still in love with Valene, no matter how many fabulous attributes his father mentioned about Daphne Charlene on any given day.

Unfortunately, Daphne Charlene liked Wyatt way too much for his comfort. Lately, she'd been finding ways to corner him, trying to kiss him or get him to kiss her, even in public. His polite deflection tactics were running low. He wasn't sure what he'd do when he ran out completely. Physically pushing her away was not something he felt comfortable doing.

Another patrol cruiser pulled into the nearly empty parking lot. Sheriff Hunter Valero, Wyatt's counterpart in nearby Old Coot and his best friend, got out of his car and approached.

Hunter had lived in Arkansas all his life, whereas Wyatt had moved down from up north, in Minnesota, when he was a kid. But that didn't matter. Everyone in Arkansas treated him like he'd always been here.

His friend took a look around at the chili-splattered folks, eyed Daphne Charlene standing way too close to Wyatt, and then Valene a few steps away. A mischievous smile shaped his mouth.

Hunter was of the opinion that when you fell in love, that was it. Didn't matter who it was, no one else would do. Several months back, Wyatt figured he'd lean on his buddy for a little moral support. Without naming Valene, he hemmed and hawed and finally confided he had a secret girlfriend. Hunter laughed. "It's not a secret, dude."

Taken aback, Wyatt said, "Sure it is. You don't know who it is."

"I do so. You're in love with Valene Grey."

He'd been shocked into momentary silence. After several quiet seconds, he asked, "How do you know that?"

"Last month I saw you two making googly eyes at each other."

"Where?"

"Baseball game."

Wyatt shook his head. "We didn't sit together."

"No. But you spent the entire game gawking at each other and sending longing looks across the field."

"Who else knows?"

Hunter shrugged. "Don't know. Maybe no one noticed but me."

"Why did you notice?"

"Maybe I did because you're like a brother to me." Wyatt knew the admission was nothing but the truth. Hunter's father was a military hero who died when his son was a baby. Hunter's mother never remarried, so he appreciated the value of family, blood or not.

Since Wyatt had four sisters, Hunter was the brother he'd never had.

"Don't say anything to anyone. Valene is skittish about anyone knowing our secret."

"No skin off my butt. I will say that you two look good together."

"Thanks."

Valene sometimes tried to distance herself from Wyatt, but if he persisted, she couldn't seem to help herself. Before long she'd be back in his arms where she belonged, if he had any say. Most days it was clear that he did *not* have any say.

Hunter joined the loose circle of Wyatt, Daphne and Valene. He asked Valene, "Did you win?"

"No. Not at all."

"Wyatt," Daphne Charlene said. He winced at her cloying tone. Good thing she couldn't see his expression, but Valene noticed and smiled. So did Hunter.

"Wyatt!" Daphne Charlene said in a tenser tone.

He cleared his throat, schooled his features and looked at Daphne Charlene.

She put an extra simpering expression in place. His back molars ground tightly together, luckily not making a noise. "What can I do for you, Daphne Charlene?"

"I need help with something." She crooked her finger at him. He did not want to go.

"Are you going to tell me what went on here?" he asked in as stern a voice as he dared. Daphne Charlene was a woman used to getting what she wanted, and she could be difficult. He pitied the few who didn't understand that about her.

She straightened. "I won the contest this year."

Behind him, someone said, "Boo. Hiss." It sounded like Valene's wily aunt, Dixie Lou Grey.

That woman could be quite a handful.

"Congratulations. Why does this place look like a chili bomb went off?"

"There were several people who didn't think I deserved the award. Can you believe it?"

Valene muttered, "And they started a food fight in revolt."

"Evidently." Wyatt glanced around the chili sodden area. "Who started it?"

"I'm sure I don't know," Valene said with an exaggerated shrug, though her tone suggested she did.

Wyatt looked down at her, fighting the urge to sling his arm around her shoulders and hug her to his side. Forevermore. He didn't even care that doing so would make his uniform chili-stained forever.

"Oh, yeah? Not one single little clue?"

Valene looked up at the sky, then to the left at the treetops at the edge of the park area. If she knew who started it, it was clear she wasn't going to tell him. That likely meant she was related to the instigator, but Dixie Lou Grey would never admit to anything even if cornered. If undeniable proof of a misdeed was provided, she'd either shrug and express an outlandish reason for her actions or clam up and refuse to discuss it further. As if anyone with two wits to rub together would buy her forgetful old lady act.

"What do you need my help with?" Wyatt finally asked Daphne Charlene.

She straightened, crossed her arms and said, "I need police protection and I want you to do it."

Valene snorted. Wyatt silently agreed. "Protection from what?"

"The angry mob."

"What angry mob?" He looked around them. Granted, the area looked like an angry mob had recently run through it, but there was currently no action here.

"The one that started this whole mess because I won fair and square." Her face screwed up in an expression of almost convincing misery and she started to cry.

Hunter, the coward, grimaced and quick-stepped away to check out some of the demolished booths.

"Okay. Don't cry." Wyatt moved closer to Daphne Charlene. "You'll be fine."

She flung her arms around his neck again. He wanted to sigh and push her away, but he couldn't. He turned his head and caught the eye of the lead judge.

"You're going to clean this all up, right?"

The man looked like he was being asked to be the sacrificial lamb staked to the ground to catch a dangerous predator.

The man surveyed the chili chaos and shook his head, a disgusted look on his face. "Well, I didn't do it."

"But you're in charge of this whole contest, isn't that right?"

The man sighed deeply. "I guess."

"That was a yes or no question."

The second deep sigh came with an eye roll. "Yes."

Wyatt looked at the vast chili-splashed zone. "I know for a fact a permit has been issued for a wedding reception here tomorrow afternoon. Therefore, when you do the cleanup you will have to ensure there is no chili anywhere. Not on the pavilion or the benches or the picnic tables or the grounds." Given the amount of chili on the grass, that last point seemed like a herculean task.

The judge lifted his arms in disbelief. "How? How do you expect me to accomplish that?"

"I don't know. Call back the contestants who made the mess. Whatever. I'm sure you'll think of something or else I tell the bride who is to blame."

"No." The man's eyes widened at the thought of dealing with an angry bridezilla. "You wouldn't dare."

"Try me."

"But it's not fair, Sheriff."

"Not many things in life are. Suck it up, buttercup."

Daphne Charlene at long last removed her arms from his person. He shifted a few steps away to keep her from reattaching herself.

Turning to Valene, he bent to ask, "Did Dixie

Lou Grey have anything to do with starting this mess?"

Valene choked out a fake cough, probably to buy time. When she finished, she asked, "I'm sorry. What was the question again?"

"Never mind. I believe I have my answer."

"What are you going to do?"

He stared deeply into her eyes, since no one was looking. "I don't know yet." He lowered his voice and said, "Meet me later. We can discuss it."

"Where?" Valene mouthed.

"Smokin' Hog. At eight." The biker bar would be crowded with folks they didn't know and was perfect for another clandestine meeting. He would have to dress down. If he went in there wearing his sheriff's uniform, the place would clear out faster than a public pool with a giant Tootsie Roll floating in it and they'd be left all alone. He'd love the time all alone with her, but she wouldn't.

Valene nodded slightly and went to join Dixie Lou and her friend Miss Penny, who were trying their level best to look innocent and failing in an amusing way. He wasn't fooled by anything Dixie Lou Grey ever did, but he *was*, however, a fool for Valene Grey. Heaven help him.

Wyatt walked toward Hunter.

"What about my police protection?" Daphne Charlene asked, following on his heels.

"You don't need it."

"How do you know?"

"I'm a good sheriff."

"If something happens to me, you'll never forgive yourself."

Wyatt stopped walking and she ran into his back. He turned around. "If someone threatens you, call the station and make a report. Otherwise, I have other places to be."

"Fine." She turned and stomped away. Good riddance. He might have to apologize later for his abruptness, but he certainly didn't want to lead her on.

"That woman is certainly strong willed," Hunter said, watching Daphne Charlene's stiff back.

"You think?" Wyatt couldn't seem to help the sarcastic tone.

"Do you really have other places to be?"

"Yeah. I need to head over to the state law enforcement headquarters gun range for my annual weapons certification." He glanced at his wristwatch. "I need to get there in the next half hour or reschedule. And today is my last day to qualify for renewal or I have to start the whole process over."

Hunter nodded. "Tell you what—I'm off in an hour or so. I'm happy to stick around and see that the area gets cleaned up."

"Not that I don't appreciate it, but why would you help me like this?"

Hunter lowered his voice. "I want to make sure you make it to your eight o'clock date tonight."

"There is no way you could have heard that."

"I read lips."

"Sure you do." Wyatt looked skyward, then said, "Thanks. I appreciate it."

"And I want you to make it to your date without Daphne Charlene attached to your hip."

"I would appreciate that even more."

"What are best friends for?"

Hunter clapped him on the back and moved to the center of the circle of booths, where the chili con-carnage appeared to be the most devastating. Putting his hands to his mouth for amplification, he shouted to the judges, "Once you get the bulk of the trash cleaned up and the surfaces wiped down, I suggest tapping the fire hydrant to power wash the grounds or the chili will become a hardened part of the landscape for the rest of the time we remain here on this Earth."

Wyatt walked toward his cruiser. Across the clearing, he sought out Valene with a look he hoped no one else noticed. She was helping clean up the area around the Cosmos Café's chili cook-off station. When he caught her attention, she sent him such a searing gaze of love he almost threw away his casual expression to race across the chili-stained ground and kiss her lips off in public the way he wanted to.

Instead, he tipped his hat in her direction and left before he did something irreparable to his fragile relationship with the love of his life.

Diesel Grey, using every silent ninja skill he possessed, sneaked down the empty hall and through the open doorway to his office. He looked over his shoulder no less than three times in three steps before going into his office. Earlier, he'd left the door ajar so he could get back in without anyone seeing him. He wanted peace, if only for a few minutes. If he could get into his office without anyone knowing he'd returned, he'd have blessed peace to work in for as long as everyone thought he was absent.

He twisted around, about to close the door as silently as possible, when someone said, "Good try, but I'm so sorry to tell you that it didn't work."

Diesel tried not to leap into the air at the sound of Axel's voice behind him. "I don't believe that."

"What don't you believe?"

"That you are at all sorry."

Axel grinned. "Well, I guess you've got me there."

"Pray tell, why are you here scaring the socks off me?"

"Two things. First is the hardest, so I'm starting with it."

"Okay. What's up?"

"Do you know who Valene is dating? In secret, I might add?"

Diesel straightened. He *did* know. The guy she was secretly dating had asked Diesel's permission to continue the relationship. Diesel liked Sheriff Wyatt Campbell, but he was a human. Their parents were *never* going to permit their only daughter to date a human, let alone marry one. He'd been putting it off, hoping Valene would come to her senses, find a nice Alpha man to date and then Diesel wouldn't have to say anything.

"Yes. I know."

"You do? What are you going to do about it?"

"Nothing. I'm hoping she might change her mind and find someone acceptable."

"Good luck with that, Mr. Procrastinator."

"Don't call me names. You haven't said anything, either."

"True." Axel shrugged. "I'll adopt your attitude and hope it resolves itself without an alien intervention."

"What's the second thing?"

"The rescheduling of the gulag ship run this month."

"Rescheduling?"

"Yes."

"Sooner or later?"

"Later."

Diesel pushed out a sharp breath. "Why?"

"Because the Royal Magistrate Guardsmen in charge are waiting an extra week for a certain high-profile criminal to be sentenced. His barrister has put in a last-ditch effort to clear him. However, as I understand things, it's such a long shot as to be nearly not worth the time. Still, the court must go through the motions for the sake of justice and the additional paperwork. Blah blah blah."

"Why don't they just send him on the *next* gulag run? I mean, they come through here every month now."

"Apparently the criminal is such a big escape risk that they don't want to wait for the next monthly run. He's broken out of three holding jails in three different protected spheres on Alpha-Prime. They don't want him to disappear before, during or after the last-ditch effort by his barrister fails. Which it probably will, according to the gulag officials I was communicating with."

"So the gulag ship is waiting around for his appeal to fail and *then* they'll pack him up and send him our way?"

"Yep."

"I don't like the gulag ship being only a week away from a Royal Caldera Forte ship visit."

"Neither do I, but what can we do?"

"We could tell them to do a better job of securing their prisoner while he's on Alpha-Prime, and then send him on the regularly scheduled gulag run next month."

Axel laughed. "Yeah, we could do that, but if we do them this favor then they will owe us one. Not to mention the extra fee I dreamed up and attached to this out-of-schedule gulag run. I mean, we make more anyway on these special runs, but instead of one or two out-of-schedule prisoners, there are a full thirty aboard. They are holding the entire flight for this extra-special criminal."

Diesel pondered. "How much more?"

"I tacked on a 300 percent out-of-cycle fee in addition to the regular fee bump for an out-of-schedule run with a full contingent of prisoners plus one who is very high profile and a flight risk."

"And they went for it?"

Axel shrugged. "Cheaper than having to chase Indigo Smith all across Alpha-Prime's outer rim where he has so many ne'er-do-well friends to help him escape his fate."

"Indigo Smith? Wow. He's infamous."

"Yep."

"I can't believe they finally caught him."

"No one can. That's why they are going the extra mile—so to speak—to keep him locked up and then moved off planet as quickly as possible, so his many Alpha-wide friends, family and fellow criminals can't help him escape. Again."

"What if he escapes before they put him on the ship?"

Axel shrugged. "Don't know, but currently they have a ten-man round-the-clock detail watching his every twitch."

"Huh."

"What do you think?"

"I don't think anything. I know you don't really need my approval because you've already accepted the run, so I'll just say…whatever. Do what you gotta do, Bro."

Axel grinned. "What gave me away?"

"I've come to realize that you have adopted the famous   ask-for-forgiveness-later-rather-than-permission-up-front philosophy with all manner of difficult things."

"Have I? Is this the only example of my new philosophy? Or do you have other examples?"

"I do have at least one other."

Diesel rounded the corner of his desk, sat down and pulled out the bottom drawer to retrieve a product from the latest money-making scheme wily Aunt Dixie had come up with to help bankroll what was likely the richest old folks' home in the state.

He held up the coffee cup his aunt had given him this very morning as a birthday present several months early. She'd been gleeful over his reaction when he opened the gift. She'd even had Juliana film him to capture his horrified digital expression forever.

Axel looked at the cup, but didn't seem too upset.

"I can see by your smile that you already recognize this product."

His brother shrugged. "I can neither confirm nor deny—"

"Save it."

"What's wrong? It's just a coffee cup."

"Oh, this is not 'just' a coffee cup. Do you know what happens when you fill it with a warm beverage?"

Axel said, "I can neither confirm nor deny—"

"Stop. I can't believe you approved using alien technology for one of her schemes."

"Yeah, because Aunt Dixie came to me with her latest idea, explained every intricate detail and then let me offer my opinions throughout the whole process." Axel rolled his eyes and shook his head at the outlandish idea of Dixie Lou Grey asking anyone's permission to do exactly what she wanted to do at any given time of the day.

Diesel sighed. It was as he suspected. Axel knew all about Dixie's cup caper, but still didn't squeal on their aunt.

"Fair point, but the second you saw this cup you should have come to me. You could have at least issued a warning."

"Besides the alien technology that no one will likely notice, what's your problem?"

Diesel pulled out his thermos of hot coffee and filled the cup. Seconds later, instead of an innocuous landscape with a few nondescript alien faces dotted here and there, a scandalous image of Maxwell the Martian, bare hind end pushed out like a stripper angling for dollar bills, appeared with a little thought bubble above his head that said, "Well, crack my crater, this cup is as hot as a naked alien."

The very fine detail of Maxwell's nude buttocks

as the truck stop's mascot looked over his shoulder with a silly grin in place was more than a little shocking.

Axel's eyes widened. "She gave you *this* cup?" He looked somewhat ill.

Diesel nodded. "I can't believe you knew about this and failed to tell me."

"It's not what you think."

Diesel looked at Maxwell's naked butt. "I think this is a catastrophe and we need to do a worldwide recall."

Cam burst out laughing. "No, you don't. This was only the joke cup, Diesel. Only this single cup was made, to the best of my knowledge. You know, as a joke for you especially, Fearless Leader."

"Well, hardy har har."

"I wish I could have seen your face the first time you put hot coffee in it."

Diesel looked skyward. "Get my wife to show you the short video on her phone. I'm hilariously surprised. There are even several inappropriate swear words. I'm sure you'll enjoy it."

"Thanks for the tip. I'll do that."

"Is that all you wanted to discuss?"

"That's it."

Diesel pointed at the door. "Sneak out and don't tell anyone I'm in here."

"Will do."

Axel opened the door. Nova Green strolled in as if the two had choreographed the move in advance.

"There's someone waiting to see you," Diesel's assistant said.

"Oh, hello, Nova." He put a flat hand up toward her face and said in a melodramatic tone, "I'm not the Fearless Leader you're seeking. Because I'm not really here and, besides, you also can't see me. And I'm a figment of your imagination."

"Stop pretending to use mind control on me, Diesel. It will never work and it's getting old."

"Worth a try," he mumbled. Louder, he asked, "Who wants to see me?"

"Daphne Charlene Dumont."

Chapter 3

Valene spent the rest of her day cleaning chili from the grounds of the public park. By the time she got home, she barely had five minutes to change and get out the door for her date with Wyatt at the Smokin' Hog Saloon.

Bone weary and sleepy, Valene still wouldn't willingly pass up a chance to see the love of her life.

She dressed carefully, put a sedate scarf over her head so her blonde hair wasn't instantly recognizable and left her childhood home. She took her parents' sedan instead of her two-seater sports car to additionally ensure no one would recognize her or notice where she was going.

It was Saturday night. The rendezvous location was crowded with a multitude of motorcycles and cars, including the overflowing side parking lot. She ended up leaving the sedan illegally parked on the grass at the edge of the forest next to the bar. So be it.

If they left to go to the lovers' lane at the bauxite pit, she'd insist on taking the ugly sedan. Perhaps it would remind her she didn't have permission to continue this relationship, even though her parents had hit the road again in their beloved RV after Axel's wedding.

Valene had tried to confide in her mother at the wedding, but could never get her alone without her father horning in on the conversation. Her mother, who might be sympathetic to her plight, likely wouldn't tell her it was okay to date and marry a human and stay on Earth. Still, she wished she could have told the older woman about the problem she faced.

Aunt Dixie knew. Diesel, Cam and Axel knew. If any of her other brothers knew about her secret love, they hadn't mentioned it. Dixie was the one who suggested Valene simply move in with Wyatt and not bother getting married. As she put it bluntly, "Just live in sin with your human. What are they going to do? It's only against the rules to marry one and stay on Earth. Ergo, no marriage…"

That was yet another problem. Valene didn't know what would happen if she moved in with a human without marriage. Beyond the distinct probability that her father would blow his stack or come after Wyatt with a shotgun. All six of her brothers might tag along, too. It was pointless even considering it. Wyatt wouldn't do it. He was too honorable. He'd already asked her to marry him and pledged his love for her. The sweet memory made her misty.

She held him off, saying she wasn't ready to get married, but also assuring him she loved him, because she really did. As the capstone, she said she couldn't consider his proposal until he got permission from her father to even date her. She'd love nothing more than to marry Wyatt and spend the rest of her life in his capable arms.

If only he was an Alpha.

When her father, busy RVing around the country, hadn't been available, Wyatt refused to be daunted. He went to Diesel for permission.

Just one more awkward conversation she would rather have avoided. Diesel was sympathetic, but unhelpful. Even the Fearless Leader had to follow the rules.

He'd been so lucky to discover his wife, Juliana, had a streak of Alpha blood running through her veins. Royal Alpha blood, to boot. The legend of the lost Alpha colony ship was a favorite story repeated in whispers, mostly by folks from Aunt Dixie's generation. Aunt Dixie especially was enamored of those oft-told tales of Alpha-Prime's first failed mission to colonize Earth a couple of centuries ago.

It was fortunate her brother, Wheeler, the artist in the family, also liked history and figuring things out. He found clues pointing to the lost ship while doing some online investigative work in the American northwest to discover if the humans knew anything about the ship that had crashed well before Alienn, Arkansas was established. Not that it was common knowledge, of course, or they would likely already have an alien-themed town there to rival Alienn. But perhaps there had been old stories or legends in the area about a fireball in the sky, or a crashed ship or rumors of aliens in the forest or something. Nothing concrete had been discovered as far as Valene knew, but a select few were searching quietly.

Wheeler was on the hunt to find the lost colonists. Her brother Gage, Mr. All About Science, was helping Wheeler using some sort of techie application she didn't understand. The two of them would likely not rest until they discovered any and all details regarding what had happened to the lost ship. More power to them.

Aunt Dixie was a stalwart believer in what she referred to as the Lost Colony Legend. It started with the tale of a missing royal vessel from Alpha-Prime and grew after they met Miss Penny and she told them all about her life story. She was able to give them some information about what *really* happened to the Lost Colony ship, how it had crashed well away from the landing zone and the handful of survivors only made it by escaping in a life boat. She spoke about the death of the Alpha princess after the birth of her royal child, and how Miss Penny's mother—the princess's lady-in-waiting—took care of that baby. It became her own duty, with Miss Penny watching over Juliana, the princess's great-granddaughter, now Diesel's wife.

Miss Penny had been a young child aboard that fateful ship when they escaped in the life boat. As a member of Alpha-Prime's rare shifter species, Miss Penny had lived a very long life, but said she had more fire in her belly and the will to carry on, especially after finding folks from Alpha-Prime living in Alienn, Arkansas.

Resurrecting the myth added new life to the many years of speculation about what had happened to the original craft en route to a landing zone somewhere north of Arkansas.

North America had been less inhabited all those years ago, but a later exploratory mission found the precious bauxite ore Alpha-Prime relied on for fuel was more plentiful in Arkansas. The decision was made to make Arkansas the site for the second colony trip to Earth many years after the doomed first ship.

Miss Penny's mother, Paladin, did the best she could to raise Juliana's mother when the only other adult survivor of the crash, a Royal Magistrate Guardsman, Lukas Marek, didn't return from a scouting mission to find out how much off course they were from their original trajectory.

During the landing, the life boat's navigational equipment had been smashed beyond all recognition.

Paladin had been forced to move the infant princess and Miss Penny away from the landing site after a storm destroyed their meager shelter, eventually making a life for them hidden among the humans. She'd left coded messages at the landing site in hopes Marek would find them, but he never had.

Valene snorted at herself for getting lost in thoughts about Miss Penny's adventures. Clearly, Aunt Dixie wasn't the only one intrigued by the Lost Colony Legend.

The loud, lively music that spilled out of the Smokin' Hog Saloon as the door opened to admit two bikers shook Valene from her reverie about her alien ancestors, the Lost Colony ship and the Alphas' intriguing past on Earth.

A glance at her watch said she'd been sitting in the car for almost ten minutes. Time to go.

Valene pulled the scarf from her head and dropped it on the front passenger seat. She dragged her feet as she made her way into the bar—not because she didn't want to see Wyatt, but because she was going to have to distance herself from him. Again.

Maybe for good this time. There was no future for them if he wasn't willing to live in sin for the rest of their lives, and maybe not even then.

Wyatt nursed his beer while he waited for Valene to show up. He hoped she wouldn't stand him up. Vee was probably miffed that Daphne Charlene had been hugging and crying all over him at the chili cook-off debacle.

Hunter had called to report that the park looked pretty good given all the chili that went airborne. Wyatt asked if the bride was going to think it was cleaned up well enough and Hunter snorted. Wyatt made a mental note to expect a heated call tomorrow. He shook his head. It amazed him the way people acted up sometimes, when civil conversation would be a better solution to most of the issues folks faced. But no one asked him.

He shifted in his seat, watching the door as two more bikers joined the din of the crowded bar. It wasn't karaoke night, but it was crowded. Wyatt tipped his beer to his lips again, and darted a look at the door in time to see Valene pause just inside, searching for him. He resisted the urge to wave his arms and call attention to himself because she wouldn't like it.

She'd find him. She always did. And she would be much happier if he didn't do what he wanted, which was race across the room, grab her and drag her back to the booth, kissing her silly along the way.

Her gaze landed on him. He winked and she smiled. Gorgeous.

Valene skirted the edge of the dance floor and dodged several other patrons until she reached his table. He noted all the men whose eyes followed her progress through the bar. Wyatt stood up to greet her when she got close, satisfied to see those same men disappointed to learn she was taken. He had no doubt she could have anyone she wanted. He was a lucky guy. If only she wanted him on a permanent basis.

To that end, he had something new to add to his proposal. And he did plan to propose, again. And again and again, as many times as it took for her to say yes. The way she looked at him told Wyatt she wanted to marry him, but something was holding her back. He wished he knew what it was.

As if reading his mind, Valene stood up on her tippy toes and kissed him. Hands on her waist, Wyatt held her close for a few moments to ensure everyone in the place knew she was here with him and not looking for a date.

Valene broke the kiss and smiled. "Claiming your territory again."

"You got that right."

She pulled away and sat down in the booth across from him. He took her hand across the top of the table.

"What can I get you to drink?"

"My usual."

That meant root beer in a brown bottle that looked like she was drinking actual beer. The bartender looked his way and nodded when Wyatt pointed to Valene. He'd arranged her beverage choice in advance. A waitress brought a second beer for him along with Valene's frosty, cold bottle of root beer.

"Did you requalify for your annual gun certification today?"

"Does a bear poop in the woods?"

She giggled. She always giggled when he said that. It was why he repeated it so often.

"I wish I could have watched you."

"Why? It's not that exciting. I stand in a booth and shoot at paper targets with several different weapons."

She shrugged. "I watched you shoot in a competition once." Her eyes lifted, gaze locking with his. "You looked…well, really good…you know…shooting."

"Did I?" He didn't remember seeing her at any competition recently. "When was that?"

"Three years ago."

Wyatt narrowed his eyes. "We didn't even know each other then."

She lifted one shoulder in a casual shrug. "Well, I knew about you."

He squeezed her hand, suddenly understanding something about their first meeting. She literally ran into him almost a year ago. He'd been in love with her ever since. But it seemed she'd been aware of him for longer. Two years longer. Warmth centered in his chest at the idea she'd been crushing on him for two years before they even met. Maybe there was hope for him after all.

Wyatt knew the Grey brothers had a little sister. He'd even seen a few pictures of her. His life had changed the moment he came into contact with her and looked into her eyes. He'd known in a second she'd be important.

"Did I win that contest three years ago?"

"Does a bear poop in the woods?"

He laughed out loud at her unexpected quip.

Valene flashed a grin and a few people looked over at them. The grin faded. She liked to be unnoticed. Before long, she cleared her throat and straightened, but he wouldn't release her hand. He felt his phone buzz in his pocket, signaling a text message. He refused to turn his attention from Valene, and hoped it wasn't an official call from the station.

Time to change the subject. "Did the park area get cleaned up after I left?"

Valene frowned. "It looked much better than when you were there."

"Am I going to get an angry call from the bride when she gets to the park tomorrow for her outdoor reception?"

"How should I know? It's a public park. If the bride wanted a pristine space she should have booked an inside venue. I mean, there was bird poo scattered around the place, too. Is the bride expecting all the birds to be constipated during her event?"

Wyatt grinned. "Well, can't argue with that." He tucked Valene's "inside venue" argument away for use if and when the angry bride called him.

Valene tried to pull her hand from his. "What did you want to talk to me about?"

Another buzz from his pocket distracted him. He glanced at his hip and the subtle noise.

"Answer your phone, Wyatt."

"No. I want to ask you something." Wyatt put his focus back on Valene, where it belonged. He reached into his other pocket with his free hand to retrieve the surprise. He'd planned on waiting a bit before proceeding with his plan, but found he couldn't wait to hear what she'd say.

One handed, he opened the ring box below the level of the table so she couldn't see it.

"I love you, Valene."

"I love you, too."

"Will you marry me, Vee? I don't ever want to be without you." Wyatt lifted the opened ring box into her view. Her eyes went straight to the ring. She sucked in a deep breath of shock. Her eyes widened, but he saw the joy, too. She liked the ring. Wyatt mentally exhaled in relief.

Beside their table, someone else drew in a surprised breath, but he ignored it. The phone buzzed in his pocket and he ignored that, too. Someone really had a bee in their bonnet, but Wyatt didn't care. He wanted Valene. He wanted to marry her. He wanted her to say yes. He wasn't letting anything distract him until he had her affirmative answer.

Before Valene could say a word, a familiar voice almost shrieked, "You want to marry *her*? What about me?"

As one, Wyatt and Valene turned to gape at Daphne Charlene Dumont as she virtually crashed into their table. Her incredulous, outraged expression said louder than her demand that their secret love affair had been busted.

This was really bad. Somewhere nearby, Wyatt had no doubt a bear was pooping in the woods to confirm that fact.

Chapter 4

Valene nearly swallowed her tongue when she saw Daphne Charlene looming over their booth, wailing about her nonexistent relationship with Wyatt.

The ring in the box he'd surprised her with was so beautiful and so perfect. But she couldn't have it. Could she? No. Never. But she wanted it with a desire born of crazed love and affection for a man she could never have unless unreasonable sacrifices were made in the name of keeping Alpha-Prime's most successful way station a secret from the earthlings.

If they married, Wyatt's family would suffer, her family would suffer, he would probably grow to resent her and the strict stipulations of their wedded bliss. How long before he chose to have a dangerous mind wipe to erase her from his head for good? This relationship was impossible no matter how much they loved each other.

"I'm sorry. I can't marry you, Wyatt," she said, hating every word.

He slumped. "But you love me."

"I do." Tears welled up in her eyes, threating to spill over and give Daphne Charlene a truly good show.

"Tell me the real reason."

Valene shook her head. "I can't tell you."

Wyatt snapped the ring box shut and put it back in his pocket. As if at a loss for what to do, he retrieved his phone and studied the screen for a moment, then rolled his eyes. "Too late now," he grumbled, typing a response into his phone. He then pointedly glanced up at Daphne Charlene and back at Valene.

"I can't go on like this, Valene," he said, not using his typical pet name for her. He was hurt. She heard it in his voice and saw it in his posture. She never wanted to hurt him. Not ever.

"I don't expect you to. I know it's completely unfair."

"Please tell me the problem. I can't fix what I don't know about."

She didn't speak, just shook her head and didn't try to hide her utter desolation as she looked away from Wyatt's equally miserable expression. There was no fixing this problem, this stupid, secret Alpha-Prime-versus-human issue.

Wyatt stood up and retrieved his wallet from a back pocket. He threw a twenty on the table and signaled the bartender with a nod. Valene got out of the booth, too.

Daphne Charlene moved closer to Wyatt, but wisely didn't hug him or anything overt like earlier at the chili cook-off. Valene gave her the stink eye, but the other woman didn't move away. She just returned the evil look with a side of attitude. Valene gauged Wyatt's expression, but couldn't figure out what was on his mind. He probably wanted to ditch her since she'd just turned down his second marriage proposal.

Wyatt was tall, blond and gorgeous and any woman would of course be in love with him because he was perfect. He was perfect for Valene and she wanted him with every beat of her heart and every breath of air she inhaled.

She opened her mouth, about to blurt out that she was considering moving in with him sans marriage so they could be together, but didn't want to find out what he thought about living in sin while they faced each other in this raucous biker bar.

And especially not with Daphne Charlene hanging on every word they uttered. Valene didn't have the courage to make things possibly worse by spilling her unlikely idea.

"Let me walk you to your car," he said briskly. He took her elbow gently and guided her toward the door, leaving Daphne Charlene to her own devices.

"What about me?" Daphne Charlene asked loudly, causing several bikers at a nearby table to take notice of them.

Wyatt didn't say anything. He gave her a sharp glance, as if to say, "Do not mess with me right now." If he noticed any of the bikers watching them, he didn't acknowledge it. He just kept shepherding Valene toward the door.

Once through it, he searched the parking lot with his eyes.

"Where is your car?" he finally asked.

"I brought my parents' sedan," she said, pointing to it parked illegally at the edge of the forest.

"Hiding in plain sight again, I see," he said in a low, amused tone.

That's the truth! Little did he know it was also the problem.

"I'm surprised you ditched Daphne Charlene in there all alone."

"She's not alone. I saw her brother sitting in the corner. She'll be fine. Me, on the other hand, I'll be miserable for the rest of my life without you."

Valene didn't comment, but she was fairly miserable about turning down his fervent marriage proposal, again.

They reached the sedan and he held out a hand for her keys. Valene dug around in her purse, retrieved them and gave them over.

He unlocked and opened her door. When he turned back, Valene launched herself at him, wrapped her arms around his neck and kissed his cheek. He stiffened and didn't hug her back. Well, what did she expect? She'd just turned his second sweet marriage proposal down, this time in front of a horrid witness, no less. Would there ever be another ask? She mentally sighed, wishing for things that would never happen. No matter how many times he proposed, she'd have to say no.

"Let's go to your place."

Wyatt's breath whooshed out in surprise. "What?"

"I'll follow you home."

"And then what?"

"Whatever you want."

"I want to marry you."

"Except that."

"I don't understand."

"I know. I wish I could explain, but I really can't and I have to ask you to please not pressure me about it."

Wyatt's arms wrapped around her. He squeezed her gently and pressed his face into her neck, kissing the sensitive spot near her collarbone. "I love you so much, Vee."

"I love you, too. Come on. I'll meet you at your place."

He pulled back enough to look at her face. He kissed her hard and then nodded, adding a quick, "Drive safe."

"I will," she promised.

Valene drove straight to Wyatt's place, went past his house and parked around the corner on a dead-end street with only one streetlight. A well-trodden path passed from the lonely short road along the back of the homes on Wyatt's side of the street. Only one yard was fenced, right next door to Wyatt's. It would be problematic if his neighbor's dogs were out in the yard. Usually they were tucked in their doggie beds by this time of night.

She'd snuck along the path often enough to know the ins and outs of making her way past the five houses closest to Wyatt's place in the quickest time possible.

Wyatt's small house was just two streets over from the home he'd grown up in—his physical closeness to his family another example of their emotional closeness.

Valene locked the sedan and walked along the sidewalk before ducking into the nearest unfenced backyard. She carefully passed the first few homes until she came to the narrow passage between a tall wooden fence on the left and a chain-link fence on the right.

She stopped at the corner, searching the neighbor's yard for either of the humongous Siberian huskies in residence, but didn't see or hear them.

Scooting sideways between the fences, Valene took care to be quiet. No need to rouse the animals into a frenzy. She made it without incident and was soon standing on Wyatt's small patio next to the kitchen door at the back of his house.

Before she even knocked, she heard the chain lock release and the dead bolt snap free. The door swung open and Wyatt hooked an arm around her, pulling her inside.

She didn't have time to catch her breath before Wyatt kissed her hard on the mouth. She returned his kiss with her own amped-up attitude. She didn't know how long they stood in front of his kitchen door smooching, but when he lifted his head, she was breathless.

Wyatt hugged her tight and whispered in her ear, "What was your name again?"

"Very funny." She huffed. "It's Valvoline Ethyl Grey. Stop asking me that. You know I hate my name."

"Fine. I'll just call you Vee." His expression changed, though, hardened. "Why won't you marry me, Vee?"

"It's complicated."

"If I ask you here in the privacy of my kitchen, will the answer be different?"

She slowly shook her head, certain her expression conveyed her misery.

"Are you already married?"

She snorted out a startled laugh. "No."

"Locked in an arranged marriage like your brother?"

"No."

"You have another boyfriend tucked away somewhere?"

"No! Absolutely not!"

"Then why is it complicated?"

"Because…well…" She sighed loudly. "Because it just is."

Valene didn't know what to tell him. If she told him the truth, she'd have to run and get the Defender weapon out of the glove compartment of her parents' car and shoot him…again. He'd be fine, lose nothing more than a bit of time. But she didn't want to do it.

During the whirlwind wedding plans for her brother Axel's arranged marriage, Wyatt was shot with a Defender when he found and sedated an escaped animal native to Alpha-Prime near the bauxite pit's lovers' lane.

Valene had hoped Axel wouldn't erase Wyatt's recent memories, but it hadn't worked out that way. She'd had to do quite a bit of explaining when Wyatt lost forty-five minutes of memories that night instead of just ten.

The Defender looked like a hand-sized megaphone since her brother Cam—who was in charge of security for both the upstairs and downstairs businesses for the Big Bang Truck Stop—had modified the design to a compact one for everyday use.

She usually carried the smaller version in her purse, because Cam insisted on it as standard protocol for the family. Especially after learning Wyatt had been zapped at the bauxite pit. Once when she accidently left the small one at home, she failed Cam's surprise inspection of her purse. He didn't even say anything. He just shoved another compact Defender inside her bag and gave her a stern look of reproach. She'd stowed the extra Defender in her parents' glove box, not wanting to have to explain it to anyone.

Wyatt watched her patiently.

She waffled and waited and hoped some as yet undiscovered perfect answer would present itself that would allow her to live her life on Earth with the love of her life.

But so far, nada.

Wrapped in Wyatt's arms, trying not to explain why she wouldn't marry him, Valene had a burst of clarity. Abrupt and terrible logic. Unless Wyatt was suddenly identified as a royal Alpha alien like Juliana or some other non-Earth creature, there was absolutely no hope of them ever being together. At least not unless she forced him away from his large, wonderful family to live on Alpha-Prime with her forever.

How could she live happily ever after if she forced him away from everyone and everything he'd ever known, leaving them wondering where he was for all time? This was the problem she pondered every single day. It wasn't rocket science. She had her answer. She'd always had it. She couldn't expect him to leave his family without any notion of where he'd gone.

It was the same conclusion she always came to, but it didn't help alleviate her feelings for Wyatt. She loved him, but she had to let him go. She had to let him go...once and for all.

Valene stepped out of his arms. "I'm sorry, Wyatt. We can't see each other anymore."

He looked stunned. "Not ever?"

"Not in a romantic way."

Wyatt shook his head. "I do not understand, Vee."

"I know you don't. And I can't explain it. I do love you, you don't know how much. But we can't be together. Please don't call me or try to see me."

She took another step away. A queasy feeling settled in her stomach. This was it. No more Wyatt in her life.

"You're really breaking up with me?"

She stared at his incredulous expression for a couple of seconds and then nodded, once, unable to say the words out loud.

He put a finger beneath her chin and lifted her face up. "Please don't break up with me."

She blinked tears onto her cheeks and sniffed. "I'm sorry. I can't do this anymore. It's too hard for me."

"Well, it's hard for me, too, because I don't want anyone else but you, Vee."

She swallowed hard, her resolve weakening. But she had to be strong. She pictured the expression on his face when he learned he'd have to give up his family and move two galaxies away. He'd get the look he currently had when Daphne Charlene tried to engage him in conversation or hug him or snatch him into her clutches. Aggravated. Perturbed. Repulsed.

Valene never wanted Wyatt to look at her that way. She shook off her melancholy and backed away until her butt hit the kitchen door and they weren't touching.

"I'm sorry, Wyatt, but this is it. I hate that it has to be this way. I know you don't understand. And I'm sorry that I can't give you the explanation that you deserve. We need time apart. It's for the best."

His eyes narrowed. "I don't believe in ultimatums," he said quietly.

Where is he going with this? "Neither do I."

"I hope that you understand me when I tell you that I can't keep this up, either. Breaking up with me after I propose to you has become too painful."

"What are you saying?"

"If you are about to leave through the back door yet again for 'time apart,'" his fingers raised to do finger quotes, "...then don't bother coming back at all. My heart can't take it. I'm done."

His expression shifted to one of absolute desolation. She saw how much it pained him to say those words. Her gaze shifted to his pocket. The one that held the perfect engagement ring. He saw her looking and reached in to pull the ring box from his pocket. He set it on the corner of the kitchen counter.

"Did you like the ring I picked out?"

"Yes. It's perfect."

"I'm glad you like it."

"I love it. I just…I can't…" More tears welled up in her eyes. Valene sniffed them away and looked down at the space between them. They were less than two feet apart, but it felt like a canyon-sized gap.

"I love you, Valene. I don't know what the problem is, but I'm willing to do just about anything to fix it."

She nodded. "I know."

"Please trust me. Just tell me the problem."

Valene opened her mouth to blurt everything out. Everything. She slammed her lips shut before she did. Closing her eyes, she got hold of herself, breathing deeply in and out a couple of times to steady her nerves.

Valene opened her eyes, focused on his gorgeous face and said, "I understand. I truly am sorry." She reached behind her to grasp the doorknob, knowing that if she didn't get out of here right this second, her resolve would vanish completely.

"Please don't leave, Vee."

She paused. The vision of being with him on Alpha-Prime after he gave up everything for her dropped into her mind. His only bonus was having her as a wife, but in a completely foreign and literally alien land. Would he think she was worth it? Maybe she didn't want to know the answer to that question. What if one day he regretted the decision to be with her while his family suffered not knowing what had happened to him? Easy. She couldn't. She just couldn't do that to him or his family.

Valene found a slim shred of resolve, twisted the knob, opened the door and slipped outside without another word. She stood on the back porch for a long moment after closing the door on the only man she would ever love. Valene's heart was about to break, but it didn't hurt as much as hearing Wyatt slide the dead bolt into place.

Locking her out of his home, his life and his love forever.

Chapter 5

Diesel tried not to be annoyed, but it wasn't working. Nova directed him upstairs to the Big Bang Truck Stop's human convenience store area to speak to Daphne Charlene Dumont. He had heard of her, of course. She ran a business in a neighboring town, but he'd never met her. And he couldn't fathom a reason for her visit.

Diesel looked at the surveillance feeds before going to greet her.

Tall, willowy, and fairly pretty for a woman who wasn't his wife, Daphne Charlene waited by the registers with an expression he defined as determined.

Diesel emerged from the back hallway and the sign above his door that labeled him Fearless Leader. He walked past the Maxwell the Martian fortune-teller box end cap and down the snack aisle to greet his unexpected visitor.

"Miss Dumont?" he said when he got close enough.

She whirled to face him, a large smile in place. "Diesel Grey. Please, call me Daphne Charlene."

"How can I help you?" *Please let this be quick.*

Daphne Charlene looked over her shoulder at the clerk, moved closer to Diesel and asked, "Is there somewhere we could go that is more private? The matter I want to discuss is a bit, shall we say, delicate."

Space potatoes. This will not *be quick.*

He motioned her toward the back of the convenience store and down the aisle with the sale items of Maxwell the Martian products. Currently it was the quietest place in the store.

"Will this do?"

She looked around and shrugged, looking disappointed. She'd likely expected an invitation to the back office. Too bad.

"Last night I happened to be in Old Coot at a local biker bar of all places, and I saw your sister there with someone very surprising."

"Oh?" His heart sank. *This will be a lengthy disaster.* She must have seen Valene with Wyatt.

Daphne Charlene's expression shifted to one of innocent concern. Diesel didn't buy it for one minute. She wanted to tattle on them.

"I hesitate to say anything at all, you understand, but Wyatt Campbell proposed to her last night. He had a ring and everything."

Diesel froze in place. He didn't dare give Daphne Charlene the satisfaction of either

63

animosity or joy at the idea of his sister getting engaged to a human sheriff.

"And?" Diesel managed to say without giving any indication as to his true feelings on the matter. He hoped. Meanwhile, his mind raced with the implications of that incendiary situation. What had Valene said? Would she and Wyatt be moving to Alpha-Prime soon? His heart sank at the very idea of his only sister, the baby of the family, moving so far away.

"And, well, I thought you should also know that Wyatt and I have been seeing each other for a month or two now. I was shocked, of course, by his actions and I wanted to warn you that his affection for your sister might not be completely true. I never would have pegged him as a two-timer, but there you have it."

Diesel felt his eyebrows furrow. "You've been seeing Wyatt?" He knew the shock was evident in his tone.

She nodded, her expression an odd mix of innocent and gossipy. "As a matter of fact, I have dinner at his folks' place on a regular basis. Obviously, his parents don't have any idea about what's going on between the two of them."

"Obviously." *Did that sound too snarky?* Daphne Charlene made it sound like Wyatt was running around behind Valene's back. But Diesel knew Wyatt. Skeeter Bite's sheriff was a good guy. Either he didn't know about Daphne Charlene's feelings or, more likely, he had tried to spare her his lack of interest. Diesel had a pretty good idea that Wyatt was in love with Valene and he guessed she hadn't been able to break it off with him.

Daphne Charlene pouted. "You don't seem that upset."

Outwardly, he shrugged. Inwardly, Diesel had to consider what Daphne Charlene hoped to gain from tattling to him about Valene and Wyatt. Why would she even think he cared? To the human world, his sister was a grown woman, capable of making her own decisions. No one outside Alienn's Alpha population knew the restrictions that came with marrying a human.

His eyes narrowed on the troublemaker. He needed to be circumspect with regard to his feelings. Yes, he liked Wyatt. No, he didn't want Valene to marry a human and be forced to leave Earth to live on Alpha-Prime forever.

"I'm uncertain what you want from me or what you think I would do about this."

Her arms lifted into the air with decidedly dramatic flair. "He's cheating on your sister with me! I would think you'd want to warn her."

I don't believe you. What's your agenda here?

"Valene is well over the age of consent. She can date anyone she wants to." Not true, but Diesel wasn't going to tell Daphne Charlene that.

"But he's a *cheater*. As her oldest brother I would think you'd care enough about Valvoline to warn her about this."

"First of all, don't call her that. She goes by Valene for a reason."

She shrugged, but the smug smile on her face told him she knew his sister hated her given name. "Fine, Valene. Don't you care about her?"

"I think that goes without saying, but why would *you* still date him if you truly think he's a cheater?"

"What?" She looked stricken, like she hadn't considered this as an argument.

Diesel straightened. *I get you now, Daphne Charlene.* "You want me to clear the way for *you*, is that it?"

Daphne Charlene also drew herself up straight. "What? I do not understand what you are insinuating." *Oh, yes, she did.*

He shook his head. "I'm her brother, so it obviously goes without saying that I care about her feelings. But I also trust her judgment about any guy she dates. So if you want Wyatt to stop dating my sister, you're on your own. I'm not helping you. Maybe you should take your own advice and find someone else."

"But—"

"But what?" Diesel wanted this conversation over with. "I don't believe I can be any clearer on this matter."

The bell to the convenience store chimed, pulling his attention from her momentarily. When Diesel turned back to Daphne Charlene, the determined look had returned to her face. But now it was even more highly motivated.

"Well, if you aren't going to help, I'll have to find someone who will."

"Good luck with that."

She glared at him. "Mark my words, you'll be sorry you didn't help me."

"Guess I'll have to learn to live with making my own decisions and not butting into other peoples' relationships. I think you should do the same."

She made a disgruntled noise halfway between a growl and a groan and stalked out the convenience store's sliding doors in an angry huff.

Diesel might well regret a lot of things, but *not* helping Daphne Charlene by sticking his nose into Valene and Wyatt's relationship was never going to be one of them.

Behind him, Axel said, "That woman is a menace." Diesel hadn't heard him approach. His brother was freakily silent.

Stifling the urge to jump in surprise, Diesel said, "Truth."

"What did she want?"

"Foolish things I don't want to be involved in or discuss."

"Okay by me. Let's go back down to your office."

The two of them made their way to the basement level.

"What's up?" Diesel asked.

"I have some news."

"Good news?"

Axel shrugged. "Some of it, sort of, but also a bit of bad news."

"Of course there's bad news. There's always bad news." Diesel centered himself to bear up and hear really horrible news.

"I just got a message that our next luxury liner visit will be earlier by two days because of some celestial display that only happens once every ten years or something. The cruise director has arranged for a sighting of it to be a feature of the trip."

"You're saying that there will be only five days between the luxury liner's visit and the gulag special run?"

Axel nodded.

"Is that the good news or the bad news?" One had to be clear with Axel. His concept of good and bad was sometimes skewed.

"The bad news. The good news is Indigo Smith's appeal was denied over some sort of technicality, but what with moving all the prisoners back to the interstellar ship, it will only be here a couple of days earlier than scheduled."

"So we're back to a week between the two?"

"Yep."

"Anything else I need to know?"

"Well, solar flares from Earth's sun are up lately, but scientists don't know why."

"What does that have to do with this?"

"Nothing. Just making conversation."

"Very funny."

Axel laughed and punched him in the shoulder. "I live to please."

Diesel delivered a shoulder punch of his own, then sobered. "I hate to say this, but I have a bad feeling about this whole out-of-schedule gulag run."

"Because of the time between the two visits?"

Diesel shook his head. "No. Because of who will be aboard when it docks. I suggest you triple whatever security Cam suggests."

"Already did."

Diesel grunted. "I hope it's enough."

"You and me both."

Skeeter Bite – Two weeks later

Wyatt managed to do all the things he normally did in the wake of his breakup with Valene. He got up every morning as usual. He showered. He ate breakfast. He got ready for work. He went to his job, did the sheriff thing all day long with a fair amount of dispassion and returned home. Then he changed clothes, sat in front of his television and watched mindlessly, not really seeing anything as he considered what to do with the rest of his life without Valene. The pattern had continued for a couple of weeks. He didn't expect it to change anytime soon.

Hunter was worried about him. He blamed himself for the useless texts he'd sent that pivotal night at the Smokin' Hog Saloon, trying to warn Wyatt that Daphne Charlene had followed him there with her brother in tow. Wyatt said as few words as possible, but told his friend he appreciated the attempted warning and not to worry. He just needed time to adjust to his regular life without Valene. No one could help him with that.

His parents were also worried about him. They said he seemed like a ghost of his former self, a phrase Hunter also used. They continually asked him what was wrong and invited him over for dinner each and every night. He politely turned down their repeated requests. He did *not* want to see Daphne Charlene. However, she was a continual thorn in his side as his days and nights blew by in a blur of desolate contemplation.

Daphne Charlene had outdone herself by spreading rumors all over the county, and likely beyond, about his proposal to Valene Grey and her subsequent refusal to marry him, citing his relationship with Daphne Charlene as the reason for their breakup. It was a big, fat lie that he hadn't bothered to dispute. He just hadn't had the heart to set anyone straight over his personal life one way or the other. It was no one's business. Let them all think what they wanted. It wouldn't change anything.

It also didn't stop the annoying woman from approaching him at seemingly every turn, especially during the day. Daphne Charlene had cornered him at the station this morning, bearing a foil-covered baked sweet something special from her café, quietly imploring him to meet her at an out of the way place, or at dinner with his parents or to just simply meet with her anywhere. He turned her down and told her in as dispassionate a tone as possible to stop spreading tales about his proposal to Valene or he'd make her sorry.

Truthfully, he wasn't certain what would make Daphne Charlene sorry for anything she ever did, but if she pushed him any further, he'd do his best to find out.

Two seconds after his promise of retaliation, he found out one thing she definitely didn't like. Daphne Charlene, apparently unused to being spoken to in such a sharp manner, showed her true personality in the heated moment. She huffed, she puffed, she threatened to blow his house down if he didn't cheer up and take advantage of what she offered.

In an overloud tone, she said, "Don't you understand, Wyatt? Now that Valvoline has turned down your marriage proposal, I want to be your girlfriend, then your fiancée! I plan to marry you one day very soon. We will be the perfect power couple in this town if you would just cooperate!"

Wyatt, highly aware that his staff had just gotten an earful about the reason he'd been so unhappy, said nothing, but he may have rolled his eyes.

Unfortunately, Daphne Charlene decided this was his way of issuing her a challenge.

"I will not be thwarted. Valvoline doesn't want you, I heard her myself. I don't understand why you won't at least meet with me. It's been two weeks! Get over it! Get on with your life…with me! Lots of people have told me what a catch I am. So catch me already!"

There was not a single sound in the sheriff's office after her loud declaration regarding his failed love life with Valene and Daphne Charlene's plans for his future.

Wyatt frowned, letting her know he was unhappy with her declaration.

She didn't seem to care. "Eventually you *will* see things my way, Wyatt Campbell. Just see if you don't." She stormed out of the sheriff's station, slamming the door hard enough to rattle the panes of glass. It was a miracle it didn't shatter into a thousand pieces. Like his heart.

After his failed love life was broadcast to his staff with as much delicacy as the cover story in this week's gossip news tabloid, Wyatt retreated to his office, expecting that no one would dare bother him unless the place was on fire. He was right. They left him alone all day.

At the end of a long, quiet workday, Wyatt still didn't care about any repercussions that might come from his lack of interest in a relationship with Daphne Charlene or her threats. He was numb through and through. He saw his life as a lonely tableau of endless, isolated and joyless days until he died, alone and miserable at long last.

As the staff had after Daphne Charlene's shocking announcement, Hunter had left Wyatt alone for a time, too, but called to guilt him into joining a few of their buddies for the monthly poker night in a few days.

Wyatt said he'd think about it, but he had no intention of going. He wasn't ready to face the world without the possibility of Valene being part of his life. At least not yet.

He watched his television, torturing himself with memories of each and every moment he'd spent with Valvoline Ethyl Grey set on a repeating loop in his mind.

The sharp knock at his door startled him out of his funk. He almost ignored it, but then a series of speedy blows on the solid wood came again, along with a muffled voice that sounded like Valene's brother, Diesel.

Wyatt peeked out the front window to see Diesel's truck parked behind his vehicle.

"Wyatt! Are you in there?"

Wyatt snatched open the door. "What's up?"

"I need your help."

Wyatt was about to say, "Of course, whatever you need." Then he noticed Valene standing behind Diesel. He spoke without thinking. "What's *she* doing here?"

Diesel's expression remained civil even as disapproval flashed across his face. "She was the one who told me where you live so that we could come get you."

Wyatt glanced at Valene's beautiful face. She looked as miserable as he felt. "Valene," he said curtly.

"Wyatt," she responded in an equally brisk tone. He didn't know how she could be more beautiful than he remembered. Valene looked like she was trying to be stoic, but her lip trembled before she turned away, heading back to Diesel's big SUV.

He was still clueless as to why they couldn't be together. But he wanted her even more, as if the past two weeks had only made his love for her grow with an out-of-control exponential force.

Diesel started talking. It took a moment for the urgent tone of his voice to penetrate Wyatt's distraction. "Wait. What are you saying?"

Diesel let out an impatient growl and repeated, "There's been an escape. I need you to help me track down some prisoners in the woods outside of Alienn."

"A prisoner escape?" Wyatt looked toward his police radio on the desk tucked in the corner next to his dining room table and wondered why this was the first he was hearing of any kind of prisoner escape. "Federal, state or local?"

Diesel started to say something, but stopped. Then he said, "None of the above. It's…well…*other*."

"Other?" Wyatt went to the hall closet where he kept his gear. Automatically, he grabbed his jacket and badge and retrieved his gun from the locked safe on the top shelf. His mind raced trying to understand the word *other*. "Like a foreign escape?"

"That's closer." Diesel motioned Wyatt toward his SUV as he locked his front door. "I'll explain everything once we get back to Alienn, okay?"

"Okay." Wyatt had no idea why he was going along with this. As sheriff, his first response should have been to check in with the deputies on duty to see if any notices had come into the station. Instead, he'd grabbed his stuff and followed Valene's brother out the door.

"Cam's riding shotgun. Hop in back with Valene, okay?"

Oh no. "Um…okay." Was this about to be some sort of comeuppance because he and Valene had broken up? Would he be surrounded by all of her brothers once they reached Alienn and forced to explain why she looked so miserable? Did they not know he was miserable, too?

Wyatt climbed into the back seat of Diesel's big, black SUV where Valene was already putting her seat belt on. He asked in a low voice, "What's this all about?"

She didn't look at him, staring at the space on the seat between their legs. "You'll see. And then you'll understand everything." The last part of her sentence was said in a whisper, but he heard her.

Cam Grey nodded at him from the shotgun seat in front. He didn't look particularly angry to Wyatt, but definitely worried about something.

They drove in silence for several minutes until Wyatt started seeing the billboards for the Big Bang Truck Stop and Maxwell the Martian as they reached the last five miles to Alienn.

Diesel pulled into the main parking lot of the Grey family's Big Bang Truck Stop, but parked around the side near an employee entrance gate to a fenced-in area at the back of the convenience store. The four of them exited the SUV as the gate opened.

Axel Grey stepped into view. He noticed Wyatt and asked, "Hey, Wyatt. Ready to go down the rabbit hole?"

Wyatt's lids narrowed. "I'm sorry. A rabbit hole? What does that mean?"

"We haven't told him yet," Cam said.

Axel rolled his eyes. "What are you waiting for?"

They all stepped through the gate and into the fenced-in area. Wyatt noted it was actually a very solid-looking metal door. There was a clicking sound as some mechanism bolted solidly in place behind them.

"To get him behind a locked door so he won't be able to run away screaming when he finds out what we all are." Valene stayed well out of Wyatt's reach as she answered Axel, but her attention was on Wyatt.

"What you all are? What do you mean?" Wyatt didn't get what was going on. Abruptly, a horrible thought occurred to him. Were they felons, hiding in plain sight at a truck stop to keep a low profile?

"You aren't about to tell me you all run some sort of criminal enterprise, are you? Because friends or not, I will arrest you." Wyatt's tone was light, but he wasn't kidding.

"We aren't criminals. We're aliens." Cam stared at him. They all stared at him, waiting for a reaction.

"Aliens," he repeated. Not a question. A statement. That was not at all what he expected. "Like from another country?" he ventured a guess, but his sixth sense told him that was not at all what they were saying.

"Nope. Like from another galaxy. We are from the planet Alpha-Prime, two galaxies away." Diesel stood tall, arms crossed, his expression expectant.

"Another galaxy. A planet called Alpha-Prime." Wyatt looked at each of them, a smile poised on his lips as he waited for the punch line. His fledgling smile died as their expressions remained serious. Apparently, they weren't kidding. "So, are you all hideous, slimy creatures with a dozen tentacles, but you've taken on a human form to hide in plain sight here on Earth?"

"Not all of the species from our galaxy have tentacles or are slimy. Alphas are humanoid, but we are taller and stronger than the average earthling, plus many of us can read human minds."

Wyatt laughed. This was crazy. "You can read my mind. Sure."

Diesel turned to Cam. "I'm not good at it, but Cam is."

Wyatt tilted his head to one side and eyed Cam. The other man seemed preoccupied, as though studying something complex.

Wyatt was about to tell them to let him in on the joke when Cam said, "The only thing on your mind beyond what we've just told you...is Valene. For almost a year now."

Wyatt lifted one shoulder in half a shrug. "I like her. That's not a secret, is it?"

Diesel didn't smile as Cam continued, "When you are alone together, you call her Vee."

Wyatt's eyes widened.

"Cam! Stop it." Valene sent Wyatt a miserable, wounded and betrayed gaze.

"No. He needs to understand, Valene."

Valene crossed her arms and looked forsaken.

Wyatt took a single step closer to Cam, staring

him in the eyes with a particular thought in his head. "What am I thinking right now?"

A half smile shaped one side of Cam's mouth. "Daphne Charlene Dumont makes your skin crawl every time she talks to you and especially when she touches you."

"That's right," Wyatt said. "And it's the truth, too."

Cam looked at his sister. "You asked Valene to marry you, but she turned you down and broke your heart, right in front of Daphne Charlene, and now the woman who makes your skin crawl won't leave you alone."

"Cam!" Valene warned.

Wyatt nodded. "True again."

"I'm so sorry, Wyatt." Valene's soft tone hit him at a visceral level. He took a step in her direction.

"Now that I know the truth, will you say yes?"

Diesel inserted himself between them. "No."

Cam continued, "You also want more proof. You want to see a spaceship or a slimy creature with tentacles."

Wyatt nodded. "Very good. I'll definitely have to guard my thoughts around you."

Diesel said, "You're taking this pretty well, Wyatt."

"Not really. I'll wake up in a minute. I'm probably asleep in my chair in front of the television after watching the SYFY channel." *But this doesn't feel like a dream.*

"It's all true, Wyatt. It's why I can't marry you," Valene said. "If I say yes to your proposal—and I really want to—then we'd have to move to Alpha-Prime and live there for the rest of our days. Your family would never be told where you were. They would have to live with your unexplained disappearance forever."

Valene sent him such a look of longing, he took another step in her direction. Diesel also took a step closer. He looked grim about the whole situation. Whether the escaped prisoners or Wyatt and Valene's heartfelt relationship was his primary concern remained a mystery.

"This is all really charming and everything," Axel said in an uncharacteristically snarky tone. "But we have fifteen escaped prisoners on the loose as we speak and we need to go after them!"

Diesel grabbed Wyatt's arm, keeping him from moving any closer to Valene, and asked, "Will you help us?"

"Of course. What do you want me to do?"

Cam and Axel shared a look. *Can they talk telepathically?*

"No. We can't talk telepathically," Cam said. "We're just brothers."

I still haven't seen the spaceship. If there really is one, Wyatt thought hard as he stared at Cam.

Cam rolled his eyes. "Let's show him the ship the prisoners escaped from and then he can help us track the ones who got out of the building."

Would it do any good to tell you to stop reading my mind?

"No. But I'll make a special effort to stay out of your head, given that I don't want to be treated to any more images of you kissing my sister. Gross, dude." Cam went to a wide door at the back of the building.

Wyatt shook his head, still half ready to believe this was all a dream. He winked at Valene and followed Cam. Valene, Diesel and Axel trailed him. On the other side of the door, a set of normal-looking stairs led down. Interesting. Most structures in this area didn't have a basement. The water table was too high. As he descended the stairs into a rather cavernous space, he noted there was not a speck of water in sight. He followed Cam to the left as they walked into a long, large room. Wyatt tried to get his bearings. He figured the large underground space extended behind the truck stop and possibly into the woods.

It looked like an underground mall. There were eateries, shops selling all manner of earthly goods and kiosks filled with trinkets and baubles.

They passed a store window that displayed every type of Maxwell the Martian paraphernalia he'd ever seen in one place, save the truck stop's gift aisle upstairs.

Wyatt never would have believed there was such a large underground area under the truck stop if he wasn't seeing it with his own eyes. They continued down the central walkway toward a platform against the wall at the end of the cavernous space. Two staircases led off the platform, one a little grander than the other.

"You're exactly right. One is for first-class passengers, the other is for everyone else." Cam didn't bother looking contrite for reading his mind and Wyatt decided it would save time to ignore any intrusions into his mind.

"What is this place?"

"This is where the spaceships' passengers disembark."

Cam headed for the non-first-class stairs, went up them and opened the door to outside. Wyatt reached the top of the stairs and crossed the threshold. He saw the spaceship immediately. It was dark outside, but the large black ship—which hovered several feet above the ground—looked like some sort of alien battleship with metal plating and gun turrets in strategic places. The ship's lights were purple, green, blue and dark pink. Four thick metal chains ran from beneath the ship to hook onto iron rings driven into the ground. A piece of equipment that looked like movable airport stairs was snugged up to an open door on the alien spacecraft.

Behind the hovering ship, Wyatt saw the woods he'd learned tracking skills in as a kid. Never once had he ever seen any alien ships hovering around anywhere.

"How do you keep it from being seen by anyone on Earth?"

"Alien technology. It blocks any kind of human radar and field dampeners keep local earthlings from seeing anything except what they expect to see."

"Right. What happens if someone does see it?" Wyatt did his best to curb his fantastic thoughts regarding aliens being in his life without his knowledge all this time. Even in his mind he likely sounded like a hayseed from the hill country, wide-eyed and awestruck by the thought of proving aliens truly existed.

"We have to erase their memories."

"Erase memories? You can do that?"

"Yes." Cam pulled what looked like a megaphone the size of a small water gun out of his pocket.

"I'm going to set this for ten seconds." Cam pointed it at him.

"Don't, Cam," Valene's impassioned voice said.

Wyatt's vision went black for a full count of three. When the black screen in his brain faded, he couldn't remember what he'd just said. What had they been talking about? The awesome spaceship?

"How do you keep the ship from being seen by the locals?"

Cam wore a Cheshire grin. He gestured with the small megaphone in his hand. "I shoot you with this and you forget. In fact, I just did it."

"You erased my memory?"

"Yep. Only ten seconds' worth, though."

"This time," Valene said under her breath.

"This time? You've used this on me before?"

"Not me. Axel blasted you the last time," Cam said, his tone matter-of-fact, like erasing memories was standard practice. From the sounds of things, it was.

Axel sent his gaze to the sky, shaking his head as he dropped it to stare at everyone with a hostile expression. His agitation was clearly visible in his posture. "Focus, people. Fifteen escaped prisoners, remember? We should already be out there looking for them."

Diesel asked Wyatt, "If you were about to look for fifteen escaped prisoners from the gulag prison ship you see here, what would you need to know to track them down in the surrounding terrain?"

Of course. He should have realized that was why they needed him—he had experience with tracking and knew these woods like the back of his hand. Or thought he had. Wyatt considered. "How long have they been gone? Are they wearing shackles or handcuffs that might slow them down? Do they have any weapons? Have any calls gone out to the local population for sightings?"

"Almost an hour. No. Not that we know of, but it's possible they appropriated weapons during their escape. And absolutely not," Axel said.

Wyatt thought about slimy tentacles. "Are they all humanoid like you?"

"No."

"Okay. Any aliens with super-human speed or the ability to go through woods faster than the average human?"

"No."

Wyatt pondered his options for only a few seconds. "Unshackled in this terrain for nearly an hour, assuming no one on the highway has picked up any odd hitchhikers, we're looking at a five- to seven-mile radius from this location as a primary search area.

"The bulk of the search area is forested. That's lucky, as it will slow them down, hopefully, but it also complicates things, as there are likely thirty or more cabins, homes, barns and various structures of all sizes, some abandoned, most not, within that same area."

He pointed to Cam's memory wipe device. "I suggest every search group carries one of those mind wipe things just in case any other civilians are involved."

The familiar acerbic half smile shaped Cam's lips. "Already set up. I like the way you think, Wyatt."

"Well, you have a front-row seat on that score, don't you?"

"True. But I'll endeavor to stop."

"We don't have to shoot to kill, do we?" Wyatt asked, wondering if he'd have to shoot slimy aliens with tentacles, and what part of the creature he should aim for. Where were their hearts? Did they even have hearts?

"No, of course not. We aren't barbarian aliens. We have rifles and guns with alien tranquilizer pellets. Sort of."

"Sort of pellets? What do they do?"

Cam lifted the rifle off his shoulder by the strap. "It's something new I invented for just this eventuality. The pellet is soft and when it hits the target it splatters the alien treatment, if you will, in a wide pattern. The drug must touch the skin to have any effect."

"What does this *treatment* do?"

"It calms the prisoner and makes them suggestible. They must do whatever is asked of them."

"So you can calmly ask them to get back into their holding cell and they go willingly. Right?"

"Exactly. My initial design was in the form of a sticker. We had to get close enough to attach the sticker to the skin of our target, and that can be risky."

The slim shred of a memory came into Wyatt's head. "Is that what you used on the wild dog you chased through the countryside a while back?"

Cam nodded. "Took three stickers to get that beast calmed down enough."

"Did I help you track it down back then?" Wyatt asked.

"Yes," Diesel said. "You did help us."

"But I can't remember because—"

"Because we shot you with the Defender afterward." Diesel gestured to the megaphone in Cam's hand. "And I'm sorry, but we'll have to erase your memories after this adventure as well."

Wyatt eyed Valene.

"Have *you* ever shot me with a…Defender?" he asked.

Valene shook her head.

"Something strange happened a few months ago, where I'm sure I lost time. You tried to explain, and distracted me, but it never truly made sense."

Axel nodded. "Yeah, that was me. Sorry. The Defender was set for forty-five minutes. I didn't mean to erase your memories for that long."

"I lost forty-five minutes?" Wyatt looked at Valene, who looked even more miserable.

"No time for that now," Axel said, handing Wyatt one of two alien tranquilizer rifles he held, along with two extra magazines of alien ammo. "We need to catch the alien prisoners. I already know you're the best shot we have on this team."

Wyatt's head spun with data and questions, but he concentrated on the rifle. He pulled the weapon to his shoulder, flicked off the safety, looked through the scope to target a nearby oak tree and fired. The pellet that hit the tree trunk splatted some sort of slimy purple substance in a four-inch circular pattern.

"Why did you do that?" Cam sounded miffed that he'd wasted a shackle bullet on a tree.

"I needed to know how this weapon fires and what to expect when I shoot it. I figured you didn't want me to test it the first time I fired it at a prisoner on the loose."

Cam relaxed and nodded. "Right. Good. Sorry. That was a great idea."

Wyatt felt completely comfortable in this scenario even with an alien weapon at his side. He slung the rifle over one shoulder by the handy strap and followed the brothers Grey—and his alien love, Valene, heaven help him—out into the forest behind the Big Bang Truck Stop to help stop a purported alien prisoner invasion.

Before they deleted his memories, he wanted to talk about the conditions that would be required to marry Valene and find out what Alpha-Prime was like. He just wished he'd be able to remember it after.

Maybe if he repeated the information over and over in his head as they zapped him a fragment of his love for Valene would remain. He couldn't imagine ever forgetting her. Then again, alien technology had already caused him to lose time and other memories. A memory he had been worried about until he realized what must have happened at the lovers' lane out at the bauxite pit.

Valene had tried to assure him they'd been kissing for quite a long time and then had fallen asleep, but he'd never shaken the idea something else had been at play. That he might have been unconscious, not asleep, but he couldn't figure out how or why.

Now he knew what had really happened. At least until they wiped the knowledge away.

If only the answer wasn't friendly aliens from another planet having repeatedly used a memory weapon on him to keep their secret.

Wyatt glanced back at Valene. She smiled, but was clearly distressed by this whole situation. And he realized he didn't even know the full truth. Was she not allowed to marry a human at all, even if he agreed to move two galaxies away? Would something more dreadful than memory loss happen if they ran away together on Earth?

One way or another, he planned to find out and weigh his options.

If there was some alien ritual he had to perform in order to marry the love of his life, he'd do it.

Wyatt smiled at her with renewed determination.

Chapter 6

Valene followed Diesel, Cam and Axel into the forest behind the Big Bang Truck Stop along with her only love, Wyatt. Wyatt held his rifle at the ready, but pointed at the ground as he trailed Diesel.

Her other brothers, Wheeler, Gage and Jack, were already searching another area. Of the thirty prisoners aboard, five didn't make it out of the cryo-pods at all. Four of the twenty-five convicts that did emerge from their cryo-pods were stopped before they got out of the ship. Jack apprehended two escapees who stopped only a hundred feet from the gulag ship to gawk at the tall trees, something that didn't exist on Alpha-Prime. Four others had been quickly found in the woods nearby and returned. That left fifteen escapees still to capture.

Wyatt seemed surprisingly unfazed after finding out the Greys were aliens from another planet. He went quickly into escaped prisoner search mode, which as a sheriff he was good at anyway.

When the others weren't watching, Wyatt sent Valene positively searing gazes. She had no doubt her looks bordered on despondent. She didn't have the luxury of being able to return his loving looks. Once her brothers had what they wanted from him, Wyatt would be treated like every other human on Earth who discovered by accident or on purpose their extra-terrestrial origins.

Valene didn't plan to watch when they erased his memories. The best she could hope for was a stolen kiss before they zapped him.

He likely thought they would only erase his memories of the search, but Valene knew they planned to go back a year. To before the day she and Wyatt had run into each other.

An event that had been a happy, but unintentional meeting. Something she should never have allowed to happen.

Valene had been casually following Wyatt off and on for almost two years before accidently plowing into him as he came out of his favorite restaurant. She considered it wishful thinking, as opposed to creepy and stalkerish. Or so she told herself.

She'd thought she'd lost him when he went into the restaurant. She'd moved to find a better lookout spot just as he unexpectedly came back out to retrieve something from his vehicle. Valene slammed right into him, her face mashed into his chest, arms wrapping around his sturdy middle. Wyatt was tall for a human, and he felt great in her arms. She was half in love with him when that auspicious and unintended meeting took place.

He kept her from falling on her butt and invited her to join him for lunch if she didn't mind eating with a member of local law enforcement.

She should have turned him down. She should have pretended to be affronted by their accidental slam into each other, but he felt so amazing in her arms and he smelled so incredibly good that whatever he'd said, she would have agreed to. She smiled and nodded before realizing what she'd done.

Luckily, he asked her to lunch instead of, say, inviting her to join his secret harem. By now she knew he didn't have a secret harem. He'd only had eyes for her since the day they met.

"What kind of details do you have on these prisoners?" Wyatt asked no one in particular. They were well out of sight of the lights from the truck stop.

Cam frowned. "What do you want to know?"

"I want to know if they have a propensity to stop and hide at the first place they see or if they will try and run to the ends of the Earth to escape."

Axel pulled out his communication device and scrolled through several screens. "Looks like six of the fifteen will likely look for a hiding place, while the other seven will continue on."

"Who else is out here looking and where are they?" Wyatt's head turned left and then right as he carefully searched the area with each step he took.

Diesel answered this time. "Jack, Wheeler and Gage are with a team east of the truck stop. We're headed west, of course. South is the truck stop and north is very heavily forested and, I hope, mostly inaccessible."

Wyatt nodded. "Right. I expect your other brothers will find any prisoners hiding in that direction more easily, as there aren't as many buildings to search. The direction we're going has probably 70 percent of the structures in the entire search grid. The north is more accessible than you think, especially when you consider the motivation the average criminal will have to escape."

Axel said, "If they finish checking their area quickly, they will head in our direction. If we have to go north, we'll do it all together."

Wyatt nodded. "Good enough." They continued through the woods toward what Valene knew was a group of five cabins. They were the closest human structures to their landing field. The cabins were likely empty this time of year after the busy summer vacation season, but it was possible a few could be occupied in anticipation of the fall hunting season.

Diesel stayed in the lead, Wyatt followed close behind him and Valene was next. Axel and Cam, side by side, trailed the group, alertly scanning the trees around them.

The first cabin they reached was small and dark. A quick check showed no one inside. The next cabin was also dark, but larger. The back door stood ajar.

Wyatt took the lead, shining a narrow-beamed flashlight all around the frame of the back door. The light reflected off what looked like some sort of slime or resin on the frame near the doorknob.

He pointed to it. Her brothers nodded, as if they knew what sort of creature might be found inside. No one seemed particularly alarmed. Wyatt moved forward without asking any questions, gun raised and ready to fire as he slowly entered the cabin through the broken back door.

Just past the threshold, a staircase went directly up from a small landing. Wyatt slowly climbed the first few steps, gun up with the business end leading the way.

Valene knew her brothers planned to let Wyatt shoot the shackle bullets at the escaped criminals because he was the best shot in three counties, possibly in the entire state of Arkansas. He wouldn't miss. If she asked whether he'd be able to hit an alien criminal with an equally alien shackle splatter bullet gun, he'd simply say, *"Does a bear poop in the woods?"*

The thought of Wyatt's funny response popped into her brain. It was completely inappropriate for the current circumstances. She had to stifle a laugh by covering her mouth as though to stop a cough or sneeze, making an equally inappropriate snorting noise loud enough to be heard by everyone in the stairwell.

All four of the men on the stairs looked at her with varying degrees of annoyance. She ignored them and vowed not to think of all the funny, charming things Wyatt did. That would occupy a lot of her thoughts.

She noticed more slime on the handrail, a clear indication that one or more of the Moogallian criminals were either inside the cabin or had been. An alien that looked like a cross between an octopus and a human could be an amazing sight if a person wasn't used to it. Earthlings were not at all used to it.

Perhaps they should have shown Wyatt pictures of the convicts they might encounter. The moment Valene cleared the half stairwell to reach the cabin's main floor, a Moogallian with all eight tentacles raised as if in complete fright stepped into the room from a door on the other side of what looked like the living room.

Wyatt didn't hesitate, firing the weapon and hitting the Moogallian in the chest through two of his raised slimy tentacles. The moment the projectile hit, it splattered a purple gel into a circular blob and all eight tentacles dropped.

"Great shot," Diesel said, moving toward the now-subdued Moogallian.

"Wait," Wyatt said in a terse voice. He took a

quick step beside Diesel as a shadow flickered in the doorway. Another convict, this one a tall, burly humanoid with dusty greenish skin, burst through the doorway holding what looked like an Earth-style shotgun cocked and ready to fire.

Wyatt shoved Diesel to one side and stepped into the line of fire as he took a shot at the menacing second alien. The shackle bullet hit him square in the face. Unfortunately, as the shotgun fell from his seven-fingered hand, a crack of sound split the air. Wyatt grunted and bent at the waist. To Valene's horror, she saw the shotgun's blast had struck him in the belly instead of its intended target, Diesel.

Valene screamed as Wyatt dropped to the floor, the shackle weapon still in his capable, but motionless hands.

Wyatt woke after dreaming Valene was upset and shouting. She never screamed or shrieked, so it was rather disconcerting, even for an obvious nightmare.

His eyes opened to find Valene's brother Gage, wearing a white lab coat, standing over him, face drawn in a serious expression.

"Where am I?" Wyatt asked. His eyes searched the room, which sort of looked like a scientist's lab. He saw beakers and Bunsen burners on a table nearby. Gage Grey was reportedly interested in science, but Wyatt had never before seen him dressed for the part.

"You're in the basement of the Big Bang Truck Stop."

"What happened to me?"

Gage looked concerned. "You don't remember?"

Wyatt's eyes narrowed as he tried to recall what happened to land him in Gage's mad scientist-esque lab.

Valene. Her brothers. The escaped criminals. Correction, the escaped *alien* criminals. The rash of recent information regarding aliens and their secrets came back in a rush of memories.

He thought he'd managed to conceal his surprise at seeing the half-octopus half-man alien quite well. He got of a clean shot with the alien weapon before spotting the menacing shadow of another presence behind the odd creature.

Diesel stepped forward as the second alien, a big green meanie with too many fingers, stormed into the room waving a shotgun. Wyatt moved without thinking. He heard the odd hollow sound of the shotgun blast and something that felt like a cannonball hit him in the belly. Valene's piercing scream followed him down to the floor. Then nothing.

"I remember now. Is Diesel okay?"

Gage nodded. "Yes. And he's very grateful. His wife is even more thankful and has promised to make you her famous kitchen sink cookies."

"Kitchen sink cookies?"

"Yes. She puts all sorts of chips and nuts and other good stuff in them. Everything but the kitchen sink."

"Right." Wyatt felt a little letdown. He'd half expected some sort of alien ingredient he'd never heard of.

"They are tasty. You might even be glad you took that beanbag round for him."

"Beanbag round?" *That's why I'm still alive.*

"Yep. But at close range I'm sure it felt like you got a thousand snake bites all at once."

Wyatt started to put a hand to his belly, but didn't touch it when the pain of the bruise registered. "Wow. That hurts a lot."

"I'll bet." Gage used a needle to inject something into the IV line connected to one of Wyatt's arms. "This is for the pain."

"Some alien concoction?"

"Nope. Plain old human remedies for you." Gage smiled. "But thanks for stepping in front of Diesel. If the bag had hit him in the head, it might have been really bad."

Wyatt relaxed, taking pressure off the pain in his belly. "I didn't even think."

"That's what they all said. You just shot the prisoner in the face with the shackle stuff and stepped into the blast. But I suspect you thought it was a shotgun."

Wyatt started to shrug, unused to praise for

doing what he would for anyone, but Valene entered the room.

"You're awake," she said, looking relieved.

"I am."

She walked to the side of the bed and took his hand. "You scared me."

"I heard you scream."

Her fingers tightened around his. "I thought you got hit with a shotgun blast after saving my brother from getting his fool head blown off."

"Ain't nothing but a thing, Vee. Don't worry," he said in a soft, casual tone as if it were just the two of them. Gage had moved away and was pretending not to hear their intimate conversation.

"Still, I want to say thank you."

He squeezed her fingers.

Diesel, Cam and Axel entered seconds later and their semi-alone moment was over.

"Hey, hotshot. Thanks for saving my life. A beanbag to the face might have altered my good looks." Diesel marched over to the side of his bed, obviously ignoring Wyatt and Valene's clasped hands. Cam and Axel rolled their eyes at the remark about their brother's good looks.

"No worries. Were you able to bring the two prisoners in?"

"Yep. Easy. The other search team rounded up six more in the Eastern sector of our search grid, so we are down to seven escapees left roaming the woods."

Wyatt looked around the lab for a clock. "What time is it?"

"Time to go back and get the rest of the alien wild bunch," Axel said. "Are you ready to go?"

Wyatt tensed his abs, pleased to find the pain was nearly gone. He sat up as Gage moved closer to fiddle with the IV in his arm.

"Whatever you gave me is working great. Are you sure it isn't some alien wonder drug?"

"I'm sure. Just good old earthling pain meds. You're good to go, but I'd wear a vest. A second beanbag shot—or a hit from any other kind of projectile—to the same area would do serious damage to your insides, maybe the permanent kind."

Wyatt nodded. "Got it." He hated wearing a vest, but would do it. The idea of anything touching, let alone striking, his bruised belly once the pain returned made him a little nauseous.

Gage detached him from the IV. Wyatt slid to his feet. He felt pretty good, all things considered. Cam handed him the shackle rifle, or rather, the alien purple goo splatter gun, as he now thought of it.

"How long have I been out?"

Cam said, "Almost an hour."

"So the search grid has moved further west?"

He nodded. "But we lucked out. Someone called in a complaint about animals foraging in some roadside garbage cans near a cabin on Old Pine Sap Road."

Wyatt nodded. "That's another mile further and in the same direction as we were headed."

"And where we are headed now, if you're up to it."

"*Are* you up to it?" Valene asked. She sounded amused.

"Does a bear poop in the woods?" She giggled, as he expected.

Her brothers groaned at the joke, but filed out of the room one by one, smiling. Gage handed him a small envelope with two white pills inside. "Take these in a couple of hours. Don't forget, okay? You want to stay ahead of the pain."

Wyatt shoved them into his shirt pocket. "Right."

Valene grabbed his hand. "I'll remind him."

He followed the group through the large area below the Big Bang Truck Stop and back out to the wooded area near the still chained and floating prison ship.

Diesel pointed to his SUV. "It'll be faster if we take the rural route near the bauxite mine." They all climbed in. Cam claimed shotgun once more and Valene sat between Axel and Wyatt in the back. All Wyatt could concentrate on was Valene's leg pressed up against his and how much he wanted to kiss her, even at the expense of her three brothers beating the crap out of him for even thinking of it.

Cam turned in his seat to give Wyatt a narrow-eyed look. "We wouldn't beat the crap out of you for just *thinking* it."

Wyatt pushed out a frustrated sigh. "You really need to stay out of my head, bro." Wyatt turned to stare out the window, pulling his leg away from Valene's.

She immediately reconnected their thighs, pushing into him, and slid her soft fingers along his jawline so he faced her.

And then she kissed him...hard. She slipped her arms around his neck and kissed him harder.

Wyatt kissed her back like three of her brothers weren't possibly wrathful alien witnesses within arm's reach of his neck.

When she drew away, she whispered, "I love you, Wyatt. I've loved you since the first time I saw you shooting in that tournament. While you are still privy to all my deepest secrets, I intend to take full advantage and kiss you every chance I get. If my annoying brothers don't like it, they can go suck a bushel of lemons dry."

The annoying brothers in question all laughed. Diesel started the truck and they were on the road in no time. Valene laced their fingers and rested her head on Wyatt's shoulder.

Wyatt had never been happier in his life and certainly not in the past two weeks. He thought about leaving Earth to live on an alien planet two galaxies away with the love of his life, knowing his family, his best friend Hunter, no one would ever find out what happened or why he'd disappeared.

The more he thought about it, the more he decided it was a viable option he should seriously consider—especially with Valene attached to his side.

The headlights of a vehicle coming up behind them occupied him for a few moments until they turned off the highway and onto the rural route. After a quarter of a mile, Diesel pulled into the drive of a nice home nestled another fifty feet into the woods.

A row of half a dozen trash cans, three of them turned on their sides with garbage strewn across the road, served as evidence that something odd had happened. While it was possible animals were to blame, it was unlikely, considering the bear-proof lids. Wyatt would have bet money only humanoid limbs and hands could open them up.

"Someone's been dumpster diving for dinner." Cam put his flashlight on the mess, following a few pieces of trash that formed a trail into the woods away from the cabin.

"Looks like they went that way."

Wyatt heard the sound of crunching leaves behind them. He turned and flashed his light in that direction, but didn't see anything. He also didn't hear anything else. He'd spent the last two weeks waiting for Daphne Charlene to jump out and surprise him. What with alien criminals on the loose, it was no wonder he was jumpy. *Stop being paranoid.*

"What?" Diesel asked.

"Nothing. Thought I heard something."

"Don't flake out on me. You're likely the only one of us that can hit our alien prisoners using only one shot. Plus, now that you've saved my life, I believe you have to keep doing it per some ancient proverb or something."

Wyatt laughed, pushing out a breath he hadn't realized he'd been holding. "Great. Don't memory erase me and I'll do what I can to keep you alive from now on."

A cloud descended over Diesel's features. He didn't frown so much as look saddened that a memory erasure was definitely in Wyatt's future, no matter what anyone thought.

A horrendous unearthly shriek pierced the night air and jerked their attention to the task at hand. Someone—or something—crashed through the woods away from them, as if fleeing a horde of evil beings. The howling continued. Meanwhile, the crashing sounds became more distant as Wyatt led the way through the trees toward the racket.

In a small clearing, Wyatt discovered what had made the horrid noises. The alien was humanoid, but with longer arms than a human, lots of body hair and claws tipping the ends of four-fingered hands. The alien was caught in a steel trap. The smooth edge of the trap's clamp, even without sharp illegal teeth, had broken through the alien's hairy skin. Its ankle was covered in orange blood. The being's eight claws were ragged and bled a dark orange substance as it tried to pull the smooth, strong jaws of the trap off its ensnared leg.

Wyatt shot it in the chest, instantly subduing the escapee. The clawed fingers went slack as the purple goo soaked into its chest hair. Diesel moved forward, using his foot to stomp on the lever and release the prisoner from the animal trap. He pointed his flashlight around the area, especially in the direction they'd heard what was presumably another fleeing convict who had abandoned the trapped furry orange-blooded alien.

Axel and Cam stayed with the shackled alien to dress its wound.

Diesel led the way further into the woods, with Valene between him and Wyatt as they carefully followed the trail of broken branches and tamped down forest floor until they came to a small gray alien half the size of the one with the fur and claws, but with a larger head. The alien panted as if exhausted and sat leaning against a fallen tree trunk, half rotted through at the other end. Wyatt thought it looked like a live version of Maxwell the Martian. Maybe it had been the model.

The gray alien put both skinny little arms in the air, hands displaying three long slim digits as if to indicate his surrender.

Wyatt shot it in the side and purple goo dribbled down its hip. The spindly arms dropped and the alien's head went back against the fallen tree trunk. It stared glassily up into the canopy of the treetops with a goofy, happy smile on his extra-small mouth.

"Why is he smiling? Does the purple goo make them high or something?"

"No," Diesel said. "The planet we hail from is very arid and hot with mostly sand on the majority of the land and super salty sea water when there is any. Potable water is scarce in most regions on Alpha-Prime and what few trees we have are rarely taller than we are. Most of the aliens who come to this planet are fascinated by Earth's tall trees."

"Huh." He looked around for any clues that other aliens might be in the vicinity, but didn't see any. "I'm going to circle the perimeter and ensure these are the only two here."

Diesel nodded. "Be careful," he said as he put a set of handcuffs on the alien's slim wrists and began to lead him back to his captured compatriot.

By the time Wyatt completed his search and rejoined the group, they had carried the hairy alien to the dirt road next to the trash cans and tied a makeshift bandage—it looked like a light gray Maxwell the Martian T-Shirt from the truck stop—around its lower leg. Orange alien blood had soaked through the fabric in some spots.

Gage, still in his white lab coat, pulled up in a green panel van Wyatt had never seen before. The Big Bang Truck Stop logo was emblazoned in colorful paint on the side, but the open doors at the back revealed what could have been the interior of a human ambulance.

Cam and Axel helped him load up the hairy wounded alien, who lay atop a makeshift gurney that looked more like a tall military cot with wheels than a medical stretcher.

Gage handed Cam the keys to get the van started. The small gray alien went into the van next at Diesel's short command. Valene's oldest brother tossed his keys to Wyatt. "You'll have to bring my SUV back, okay?"

"Sure thing."

Valene slipped her arm into Wyatt's. "I'll go with Wyatt."

Diesel didn't look elated, but didn't argue. "Bring my vehicle back to the truck stop, right?"

"Right," Valene said.

"Pronto, right?"

"We'll see," she said. Diesel expression said he was displeased, but he didn't say anything. He hopped into the van's shotgun seat.

The back doors of the van slammed shut, Gage and Axel inside, and Cam drove the van back toward the highway a quarter mile away.

The moment the van was out of sight, Valene threw her arms around Wyatt's neck and kissed him like they'd never get to kiss ever again. That might be true, so he hugged her tight, and kissed her back with a lot of enthusiasm.

He didn't know how long they kissed, but they both came up for air suddenly when they were startled by a loud sound, like someone or something crashing through the woods at a high rate of speed. Wyatt put Valene behind him and raised the alien gun, ready to shoot.

The noise died down, stopped and started up again. After listening for a few seconds, it was clear that whatever was crashing around out there was now headed in the opposite direction.

"Should we follow it?" he asked Valene. He *really* wanted to follow it.

"No. Let's go back and get my brothers. I don't want you to go it alone with dangerous alien criminals."

"Are you sure? I'm not a shy flower, you know." He didn't lower the gun, keeping it pointed in the direction of the receding noise.

"I know, but even you would agree that chasing a strange noise in the woods at night all on your lonesome is not the best use of your time."

"Maybe." He could barely hear the crashing now anyway, so he lowered his alien purple goo splatter gun and noted the direction of where he lost the sound. When they came out later with the group, they could start there.

"Please, let's go back." Valene pressed close. He

kissed the top of her head. She tilted her face toward his and he kissed her mouth gently.

"Okay."

Wyatt was in love with an alien girl. He kissed her again a little longer, but decided they should get out of here before their incandescent emotions ran rampant. He took her hand and they walked slowly back to Diesel's SUV. He glanced around as he walked, searching for any sign of more aliens hiding and possibly watching them from the tree line.

Maybe the smart ones had scurried away, or perhaps they watched to ensure he and Valene were really leaving the area.

Either way, he couldn't shake the feeling that someone, or something, kept track of them as they departed.

Wyatt raced Diesel's SUV back to the truck stop as fast as possible, a little unsettled that they weren't done with their search for escaped alien criminals, wishing he'd gone ahead and chased after the noise crashing through the woods.

A glance at Valene made him reconsider. He was thrilled to be finally in on Valene's big secret. It was a doozy, but oddly not disquieting. Nowhere near some of the guesses he'd pondered, for example: mob-like criminal enterprise or witness protection family a discovery away from being moved to another city. Aliens from another planet had not been on his list of possibilities.

Alien or not, Wyatt loved Valene and the idea of moving two galaxies away to be with her forever was growing on him.

Chapter 7

Valene and Wyatt made it back to the truck stop in record time. She didn't know what had been crashing around in the woods, but was grateful Wyatt didn't want to discover what or who it was all on his lonesome.

He'd barely parked the truck before hopping out to tell her brothers what they'd heard.

Wyatt sounded uncertain as his tale wound down. "Should I have chased the unseen someone?"

"No," Diesel and Cam said at the same time.

"Too dangerous all alone," Cam explained. "We need to operate like we did earlier in groups of no less than five. Trust me, you did the right thing. We'll start there when we go out again if we don't get any better information as to where they are."

Cam held up his digital tablet. "We've reviewed the bios of the final five escapees. Indigo Smith and two of his favorite lackeys are still loose, along with two more like the hairy alien we captured earlier. It's likely they've gone north, as it's the least viable path, but also the one without people. We don't know if they are all traveling together, but it's possible."

Diesel huffed. "We aren't that lucky. I'd be willing to bet a paycheck that Indigo Smith and his minions are nowhere near the two hairy beasts from Galdaren."

"Indigo Smith doesn't have anyone on Earth to help him, does he?" Axel asked as if just now coming up with that odd query.

"How could he?" Diesel didn't seem convinced it wasn't possible.

"I don't know, but I'm with Axel," Cam said. "Indigo Smith seems to be able to do the impossible. Maybe we should check into an Earth connection." He sounded especially on edge. It made sense, as he was the one in charge of security for the Big Bang Truck Stop, both upstairs and down.

Cam took his duties very seriously. "I mean, how is he loose and missing from the gulag ship where none of the prisoners were supposed to wake from their cryo-sleep chambers until arriving on XkR-9, the miserable gulag planet?"

Axel raised his hand in a semi-shrug. "It's entirely possible that it was because of the excessive solar flares."

"Excessive solar flares?" Diesel's eyes narrowed. "Didn't you say something about that a couple of weeks ago?"

"I did. I just didn't think you were listening." Axel managed a half smile, then sobered.

"Speculation from Alpha-Prime is that excessive solar flares from the sun, apparently a common occurrence here, never happen in our galaxy and they've somehow messed with the operation of the cryo-pods carrying the alien prisoners."

"Somehow messed with?"

"Okay, interfered. As in rendered the cryo-pods useless by spontaneously generating an out-of-cycle system check that rebooted each cryo-pod, allowing every one of the prisoners to thaw, wake up and for most of them escape. As a bonus, it also prevented the few guards tending them from accessing the information on their digital security devices until prisoners were racing past them into the woods behind the truck stop."

Gage raised his hand. "I thought only some of the pods popped open."

"Nope. Every single one opened up, but some of the prisoners—depending on their physiology—were more easily able to shake off the drugs from the cryo-freeze process. A handful never even made it out of their pods."

"Not to be defeatist, but the only prisoner of the remaining five that I'm worried about is Indigo Smith. He's smart, wily and could easily charm a little kid into giving up his whole stash of Halloween candy without the child shedding a tear."

"Here's a question," Wyatt said. "Why aren't the guards on the prison ship helping us search for the escapees? You'd think they would be prepared for this kind of thing."

"Since the prisoners were supposed to be safely slumbering in cryo-pods, only three guards accompanied the ship," Diesel explained. "They're needed to guard the recaptured prisoners. Besides, none of them have ever been to Earth before. We're better equipped for a ground search than they are."

Wyatt nodded. "Makes sense. Are we going back out tonight?" he asked no one in particular.

He squeezed Valene's fingers without looking at her. No one had noticed them canoodling and Valene was grateful. She hoped she could go back to Wyatt's home and explain everything. Even if he didn't get to remember it later. At least they could talk and discuss various *what if* scenarios. Then, once his memory was gone, she'd know what might have happened. A pain in her chest registered what it would be like to see Wyatt after his memory wipe. She shut that thought down. It was too painful to think about. If he lost his memory, she would be wise to never try to see him ever again. That made her eyes water. *Stop it. Be positive.*

Gage straightened from his hunch over a computer terminal a few feet away. "Hey! I just figured out a way to track the remaining prisoners."

"How?" Cam said, already moving toward Gage.

They all crowded around his terminal. "The chemical drugs they use in the process to prep the cryo-pods are alien to Earth." Valene heard someone snicker, probably Axel.

"Meaning what?" Diesel asked.

"Meaning that the substance doesn't occur here on Earth, so it's easy to spot."

"Say it again in English," Axel said.

Gage took a deep breath and seemed to center himself. "Once out of the cryo-pods the prisoners' bodies will all emit this particular chemical, like a scent. It's a very unique signature. One we can track using regular satellite imagery of the area."

"Secret government satellites that you'll have to hack into at great peril?" Axel asked.

"No. Regular ones anyone can use, but I can add my own filter and search overhead for wisps of the alien chemical."

"How long will it take to set up the tracking?"

Gage shrugged. "Eight or ten hours to run it after I make some changes to my software, say another hour or two. The bad news—"

"Why is there always bad news?" Axel asked the question Valene suspected they were all thinking.

Diesel crossed his arms. "What's the bad news, Gage?"

Gage cleared his throat. "Eventually the unique signature trail will no longer be in their systems."

"What you're saying is that we have a time limit?"

"Yes."

"How long?" Axel asked.

Gage studied his computer screen as if for clarification and said, "Depending on absorption rate and the degree to which they are expending the chemical during any physical activity with the added complexity of the Earth's atmosphere..." He stopped talking as everyone's eyes glazed over. He liked to explain things, but his sister was sure she wasn't the only one who thought he often he sounded like Charlie Brown's teacher. "Waa, wanh, wanh, waa, waa, wanh, wanh."

"How long? And this time say it in ten regular English words or less."

Gage pushed out another long sigh, looked skyward and said, "I'd say a day at the most, but probably less. I won't know until I make my changes and let the program run. Ask me again at high noon tomorrow."

Diesel looked at his watch. It was just after midnight. "Let's meet here in twelve hours or rather high noon, not to be dramatic." Gage made an uncharacteristic snort as Diesel continued, "It will be daylight by then. Our search should be much easier once we find the area Gage will provide after he does his magic.

"Listen up, folks. We *will* get these last five criminals back in their pods and headed for their gulag destination well before the time the ship needs to depart." Diesel sounded as if his decree was written in stone. Valene didn't think it would be that easy, but kept her private thoughts to herself. She probably wasn't the only person in the room with the same idea.

Valene squeezed Wyatt's hand. Twelve hours to bask in his knowledge of what she'd been unable to share with him for a year. There would be kissing. And lots of it, if she had any input for the next twelve hours.

"Let's go to your place," Valene whispered.

Wyatt looked deeply into her eyes and nodded slightly. He released her hand and put his arm around her shoulders, pressing her to his side. Valene melted into him, slipping her arm around his waist.

They started to leave. Diesel moved to block them.

"Where are you two going?"

"None of your business." Valene wasn't going to be thwarted. She and Wyatt deserved time alone to discuss the revelations of this evening.

"Why don't you both stay in Alienn?"

Wyatt opened his mouth, but Valene spoke first. "No. Thanks, Diesel. We'll be back at noon tomorrow ready to hunt down the remaining criminals."

Diesel pushed out a tired-sounding sigh. "Fine." He looked at Wyatt. "It goes without saying that you will not discuss any of what you learned tonight with anyone else. Not family, not Hunter, not your mama in a weak moment, no one. Got it?"

Wyatt nodded. "I won't even tell Valene."

"Good." Diesel stepped aside to let them pass, but not before giving her a stern look that seemed to say, "Don't do anything you'll regret, that exposes us to the humans or that your brothers will then be forced to seek retribution for."

Valene rolled her eyes at him, knowing he hated it. He harrumphed as they left.

Valene got behind the wheel of her parents' sedan and Wyatt took the passenger seat. She drove quickly to Wyatt's home, passed his driveway and parked on the dead-end street.

Wyatt looked amused. "So we're going to sneak into my backyard, are we?"

"Yep." Valene grinned.

"I do have a key, you know. We could enter through the front door like regular people."

Valene shook her head. "I'm not regular people, I'm alien."

Wyatt only smiled.

"Besides, it's a force of habit. And sneaking in the back way will be fun."

"Awesome. Lead the way, my alien warrior princess." He unbuckled his seat belt and got out of her parents' sedate gray sedan, the total opposite of Valene's flashy sports car.

They made it all the way to Wyatt's back porch before the two Siberian huskies next door were unexpectedly let out into their fenced yard.

Wyatt was fiddling with the key in the dead bolt

as the two dogs raced to the fence line. They jumped in the air, throwing themselves against the fence, barking furiously at something beyond the fence she and Wyatt had just crossed without incident.

"Boris! Natasha!" Wyatt called out sternly. "Hush."

The dogs stopped barking and hurling themselves against the fence, but kept moving, clearly agitated. They sniffed the ground, huffing and ruffing here and there. They paced the rear fence line, whining as if to convey their unhappiness or perhaps alert someone a squirrel was loose in the neighborhood.

"Boris and Natasha? Are your next-door neighbors spies with a sense of humor or something?"

"Nope. Cartoon Network fanatics."

Valene laughed. "Even better."

The lock finally clicked and Wyatt opened his back door. He gestured her into the kitchen. Before entering, he gazed out at the darkness toward where the whining dogs still paced the fence.

"Do you see anything suspicious out there? Or anyone?" she asked.

"Nope. Probably a rabbit or something they want to chase to the ground, rip to shreds and devour."

"Ew."

"Despite their cute names, they are security protection dogs." Wyatt closed the back door tight, turned the deadlock to secure it and faced her with an odd expression.

"What?"

He took both of her hands in his and squeezed. "I'm sorry I've been so determined to bend you to my will regarding my proposal and—"

"You have nothing to be sorry for, Wyatt," Valene interrupted his heartfelt apology. One he didn't need to give her. "I'm at fault. I shouldn't have been following you around like a lovesick puppy in the first place. I knew we couldn't be together, but I just couldn't help myself. I've loved you for so long."

"How long did you follow me like a lovesick puppy?" Wyatt asked quietly.

Heat crept in her face. "Quite a while."

"Two years before we met?"

"Maybe." They stared at each other. A half smile quirked Wyatt's sexy mouth. "Fine. Okay. Yes. It was two years. Since the day I saw you shoot in that competition. I couldn't seem to stop myself from finding out everything there was to know about you."

"I'm flattered. And also stunned that I had no idea you'd been stalking me for two years before shamelessly running into me."

"That really was an accident."

"Oh?"

She nodded. "You went into the restaurant and I shifted position to get a better place to watch you inside the place, but you came back out so fast that, boom, I slammed right into you."

"I remember."

"So do I."

"Now what?" he asked softly.

Valene inhaled a deep breath and let it out. "I want to play the *what if* game."

His brows quirked. "I'm not familiar with that game."

"Sure you are. Here's an example: What if I wasn't an alien only allowed to marry another alien, even though I'm in love with an earthling?"

"I see. What if I don't care that you're an alien? What if I *was* willing to move to another planet so we could be together?"

Valene inhaled again and let the breath out. "I'd say you really need to think it through. I haven't been able to get past the part where you leave your family behind without so much as a word. How long before you resent me for making you change your entire existence and, worse, from taking you away from your family forever?"

Wyatt put an arm around her shoulders and led her to his living room. They eased down onto the well-worn sofa, a hand-me-down from his folks that had already endured a decade of five active children on its solid frame, according to a story he'd told her when she visited his home the first time.

Seated side by side with the length of their

bodies connected, Wyatt said, "I haven't been thinking about anything else since I found out why you think we can't be together, but resentment won't ever be a factor."

"Really? I don't know about that. I also have to give up my family, but at least they can visit."

"What makes you think I'll grow resentful?"

"Because of all the past failures of those who thought they could leave everything behind, but ultimately couldn't."

"I am my own man. Once I make a decision, I stick with it."

"You say that now, but the odds are not in my favor. Don't you agree the possibility of eventual resentment exists?"

He shrugged. "Once I got past the part where I was sure I'd fallen asleep watching science fiction theater, future resentment still wasn't a part of my thought process."

"Be serious."

"Okay. You're right. It would be hard, I get it. However, I love you. I don't want anyone else. Even if my memory is erased, I can't imagine myself loving anyone except you for the rest of my life. Without you, I will never marry, never have children and die alone one day slumped over in my wheelchair when I'm 108 years old."

"What if Daphne Charlene comes after you?"

"Oh, trust me on this one, she's already after me."

"What if she catches you?"

Wyatt rolled his eyes. "She won't. I won't let her because I don't like her in that way. Even if you and I had never met, I would not have *any* romantic feelings for that woman."

Valene moved closer. "What I'm hearing is that you have romantic feelings for me?"

"I *have* asked you to marry me twice."

She shrugged. "Marriage proposals don't necessarily mean romance."

"Well, they do in my book." Wyatt reached into his pocket and pulled out the ring he'd shown her at the Smokin' Hog Saloon. It was just the ring without its box. He grabbed her hand, slipped the amazing diamond ring on her third finger and said, "Pretend I'm an alien and answer a question for me."

"Yes."

"I love you. Will you marry me, Vee?"

"Yes."

"Really?"

"I've loved you for three years, Wyatt. Of course I want to marry you, if only I could."

"We're pretending and I'm an alien now, remember."

"Oh. Right. Wyatt the alien." She giggled.

"Wait a minute. Can you read my mind?"

Valene shook her head. "Not everyone is as talented as Cam. Axel can only see vague images, which he regards as useless. I can see colors and…"

She paused as if considering whether to continue. "And I can also occasionally sense a person's feelings, but only in short bursts. Also fairly useless as mind reading abilities go."

"Feelings?"

"You know, like extreme anger, hurt, love."

"Can you read my feelings right now?"

Valene closed her eyes and concentrated. "You love me. I already knew that." She moved close, kissed Wyatt and whispered, "Are you going to let me sleep here tonight?"

"Yes."

"Really?" Valene figured he would insist on separate bedrooms or something.

"Of course. We're engaged. We should sleep together, don't you think?"

"I do. I figured you'd nix any hanky-panky."

Wyatt's brows furrowed. "I never agreed to any hanky-panky."

"But we're sleeping together?"

"Yes. And that's it. I'll give you one side of my king-size bed. I'll take the other."

Valene's eyes narrowed. "How about snuggling?"

"Okay. Snuggling is fine."

"And kissing."

"Sure. Kissing is the best."

"*What if* I curl up next to you during the night?"

Wyatt smiled. "I will wrap my arms around you and protect you with my life."

"*What if* our clothes accidentally fall off while we sleep?" She batted her eyes as he crossed his arms and gave her a resolute expression.

"Not a chance."

"It could happen."

"Oh, I don't doubt that." He gazed deeply into her eyes. "Don't tempt me, Vee. My wish is to remain honorable."

"You already are, but what if this is the only chance we'll ever have to be together?"

"*What if* I don't want to play the *what if* game anymore?"

"Wyatt."

"Valene." He put his hands on her shoulders. "What if we go get some much-needed sleep, because tomorrow we'll be hunting down dangerous alien criminals through the woods all afternoon?"

Valene nodded. "You're right. I am pretty tired."

"Let's go." They stood.

Valene wanted to let Wyatt be honorable. *If only I could get the butterflies in my tummy to settle down and my heart to stop beating so fast at the mere thought of some hanky-panky.*

Chapter 8

"Settle down everyone. Let's get started," Diesel said, taking the seat at the head of the large oval table. The cacophony of voices lowered dramatically and everyone in the room turned to the man they called their Fearless Leader. Wyatt cracked a wide smile the first time he'd heard it years ago and still found the title amusing now that he knew Diesel was in fact an alien from another planet, just like their mascot, Maxwell the Martian.

Wyatt sat next to Valene in the assembled group that included all six of her brothers, plus lots of folks he would never have guessed were aliens. They held hands under the table. In his left pocket rested the ring she'd taken off right before they got out of her parents' sedan to come inside the truck stop's super-secret alien basement. Wyatt had wanted to bring his own vehicle, but Valene wisely decreed that needing to give him a ride home later not only saved on gas, but made it easier for them to be together by the end of the day.

"First of all, thank you for volunteering. I know this task won't be easy. Traipsing through the woods to the north will be taxing. To that end, I've invited some help from out of town." Diesel turned to the two men seated on either side of him at the head of the table. "To my left, many of you already know Royal Magistrate Guardsman Bubba Thorne. He's the best tracker I've ever met from Alpha-Prime. To my right, I'd like to introduce Luther Boudreaux. He's a top-notch bounty hunter and tracker from Ichor-Delta. Like Wyatt, he can also hit anything he shoots at."

Wyatt glanced down the table at Boudreaux. They nodded at each other once. The other man looked oddly out of place even given the fact this meeting was being held in a secret room below stairs at an alien way station. While he was tall and fairly well muscled like the others from Alpha-Prime, his skin tone was pale compared to theirs. Not ghost-sheet white, exactly, but like he'd been tucked away out of the sunshine while he recuperated from a long illness. His hair was dark, so perhaps that made his skin tone seem extra light.

Boudreaux wore stylish sunglasses, even inside this windowless conference room. Again odd, but Wyatt would save his opinions for once he had more information.

Diesel continued the briefing. "Ten minutes ago,

Gage was able to get his computer program to start tracking the cryo-pod signature of the escapees." He clicked a remote and the interactive whiteboard behind him lit up like an overhead projector display. A simplistic map showed the southern edge of the Big Bang Truck Stop. Two areas circled in red appeared on the map's northern edge, one to the right, one to the left, with gray dots inside the red circles. "It looks like we'll have to split up into two groups to go after them.

"Bubba and Luther will take half of the assembled team and head to the northeast. Wyatt and I will take our team to the northwest."

Axel put his hand in the air.

Diesel sighed loudly. "You can just talk, Axel."

"Why are there only four wispy gray dots on the map and not five?"

"We aren't quite sure. The three to the northeast are the strongest. The one in the northwest is very light. Gage speculates that perhaps the lone entity was the first to depart his cryo-pod. It's possible that the fifth was also released earlier than the others and his trail might have already dissipated."

Axel raised his hand again.

"Speak, Axel."

"I'm not a dog."

Diesel glared and didn't say a word.

Axel cleared his throat as if to keep his amusement in check. "I thought all the pods opened at the exact same time when the system rebooted after the solar flares. Why would some pods have opened earlier?"

"It's just a theory. That's what speculation means, a big fat guess. Gage also mentioned that the physiology of the different aliens might also have an impact on the data."

"So you don't really know?"

"Sure. Fine. We don't really know. The 'theory' is that the faint wisp is hopefully with the invisible one."

"That's a big if," Cam remarked. "The invisible wisp could be literally anywhere on this map or already out of Arkansas."

"True, but doubtful. Besides, we can only operate and move forward with what we *do* know." Diesel clicked the remote and a more magnified map appeared, the circles larger. "What we do know is that four out of five escaped gulag-bound criminals are lit up on this map. We are going after them and we're leaving in five minutes. We have two large capacity vans ready to depart. We will take as many roads as possible to get nearer to the marked areas, but the last two to five miles will be on foot depending which group you're with. Does everyone know which group they're with?"

Wyatt assessed the assembled group and realized for the first time that Valene was the only female in the room. She raised her hand. "I don't know which group *I'm* with."

Diesel nodded once at her. He then stood and walked over to Wyatt and Valene as they got up.

"Valene, I'd like you to stay behind in Alienn with Gage to help him in his lab. He's got a few more ideas of how to track the escapees once our time limit runs out."

"Why does it have to be me?" She glanced at Wyatt, her expression pained as if, like him, she wanted to spend every spare minute together.

"We have two panel vans with seating for fifteen each. With the two new additions to our team, there isn't room. That's why Gage is staying behind."

Valene looked at Wyatt again then at the others as if doing a quick count. "There are only twenty-five—"

"Yes, and five prisoners to bring back. What if all five are found by one team? We can't just strap them to the luggage rack and cover them with a tarp once we've shackled them."

"But—"

"No buts. It's not like we're sending you off to sit by the phone and wait for us. Go help Gage. Besides, we'll be in continual communication."

"Fine." She didn't sound like she meant that, but her brother nodded.

Diesel left them when someone asked a question about the terrain.

Once he was out of hearing, Wyatt reached into his pocket and pulled the ring out. "Here." He slid it onto her finger. "For today, while we're parted, we can still be engaged, right?"

Valene looked up at him, eyes watering up. He thought he'd made a mistake until she threw her arms around him and kissed him hard on the mouth in front of the remaining folks in the room. "You are so right. I love you," she whispered. Emotion warmed the center of his chest as she pulled away slowly. How could he ever let her go? How could he not follow her two galaxies away for a life together?

"Love you, too, Valene. I always will. No matter what." He didn't whisper. He said it loud enough for Diesel and several others who lingered in the meeting room to hear—although the kiss and the engagement ring might already have clued them in. Even so, no one made any disparaging remarks as they loaded into the vans for the trip north.

Valene sent Wyatt a woeful little finger wave as they pulled away from the Big Bang Truck Stop.

Wyatt quelled the urge to leap from the van, wiggling through the tiny window if necessary, so he could grab Valene up in a tight, bear hug and never let her go. Instead, he smiled, looking away from the most ardent temptation he'd ever known.

Flashes of memory from the night before with Valene tortured his mind for a few miles, but he quelled those thoughts and forced sports statistics into his head. Cam rode shotgun two rows ahead of his seat in the van.

Wyatt didn't see any need to invite a butt-kicking from a justifiably angry older brother who might be privy to what had gone on between Wyatt and his little sister last night. He'd already been kicking himself since dawn's early light for not being strong enough to resist her.

Then again, he didn't have any true regrets where Valene was concerned and what few he did harbor didn't last long. He'd come to a decision regarding their future.

Once they captured all of the escaped criminals, Wyatt would tell them all that he wanted to marry Valene even if they had to move two galaxies away to be together.

Valene watched the van with Wyatt pull away and thought about how unfair her life was in general. Then again, she would have been useless as a searcher of anything but her own feelings regarding a certain sheriff who made her heart go pitter-patter whenever he was nearby, especially when he was in scent range. He always smelled so amazingly good. Like starch, from his pressed uniform, mixed with the crisp scent of his soap and shampoo all comingled with his unique manly scent. Thinking about it made her cheeks heat up.

She shook off the memory and put her focus back on the task at hand. It was important to find the prisoners to maintain their secret here on Earth. Worse in her mind than even her horrid choice regarding a relationship with Wyatt was having the whole operation discovered, being unable to fix it easily and then being forced to move everyone back to Alpha-Prime overnight as a Defender bomb was lobbed toward three counties to erase as much of their alien existence from the minds of any humans left behind as possible. The doomsday scenario Alpha-Prime had recently introduced as a just in case setup was never far from her mind.

Gage tapped her on the shoulder, gave her an understanding smile and together they went back to his lab. He was working on another way to track the escaped aliens, using some sort of trajectory theory based on the other escapees and where they'd been found to possibly predict where the others might have gone.

Valene monitored the communications with the vans as Gage tapped away at his computer, occasionally mumbling to himself as he worked. Of all her brothers, Gage was definitely the science nerd of the bunch. He'd attended the prestigious XYZ Academy of Science and Medicine on Alpha-Prime for two years. The day he turned sixteen he'd been eligible to apply. He had his paperwork filled out a year before. It was a great honor to be chosen and Gage was the first colony student ever granted the opportunity to attend.

Of course, the family had to explain his absence to their human neighbors while he was gone. Their parents told anyone who asked, being as vague as possible, that he'd gone to help some elderly relatives far, far away. Then he'd come back two years later, having graduated and received a diploma from *far, far away* high school.

No one batted an eye, never guessing he'd been two galaxies away immersed and learning all manner of Alpha-alien science and medical things with a special emphasis on all things known and presumed regarding planet Earth and the earthlings residing there.

Their efforts to hide in plain sight in Arkansas had always been well-managed by each Fearless Leader in charge of the colony as well as the elder council, but trips back to Alpha-Prime, even for a lengthier time frame, seemed in Valene's opinion easy to accomplish.

Diesel, as the current Fearless Leader, mentioned on occasion that it was not easy, but rather a big pain in the patootie, quoting a favorite saying of their wily aunt Dixie.

The radio crackled and Diesel's voice came through. "Base Station, this is the NW group. We've gone as far as we can in the van. We're about to head out on foot. Do you copy?"

"Roger that. We copy," Valene said. She wanted Diesel to put Wyatt on the radio so she could hear his voice, but forced herself not to say those words.

"We'll check in on the hour. Has the NE team checked in yet?"

"Negative. The NE group has not checked in, but they had further to drive."

"Roger that. NW group out."

"Copy. Base Station out."

Valene pushed out a long sigh and put the radio transmitter with the gray push to talk button in the center back in its holder.

"What are you going to do about Wyatt?" Gage asked from right behind her, startling her out of her melancholy and into an immediate poor attitude.

"What do you mean?" Her tone bordered on irritable.

"It is obvious you love each other, given the kiss I saw earlier in the conference room, the ring gracing your third finger right now and the fact he told everyone in hearing range that he loved you, too."

She wiggled her finger and glanced down at the sparkly center diamond. "So?" She'd made it all the way up to a belligerent tenor.

Gage was unfazed by her insolence. "Are you going to marry him and leave Earth?"

Valene scowled. "I don't know yet. Why do you ask?"

Gage shrugged. "I would miss you if you left."

Deflated, Valene softened her tone. "I would miss you, too. But the deal breaker from my point of view is Wyatt leaving Arkansas forever and being unable to tell his big, wonderful family about where he's going and that he'll never return. He'd forever be a missing person."

Gage nodded in understanding. "Right. That *would* be difficult."

"I've never wanted him to make that choice. So instead of running away, eloping and spending our lives on the run looking over our shoulders every moment for a Royal Magistrate Guard to show up and shackle us, I expect after this prison escape fiasco, he'll have a massive memory wipe. It will not only cover the prisoner escapee search, but also the entire year of our secret relationship. He won't remember me, I'll spend my life utterly alone and die a miserable old crone."

Clearly ignoring the dramatic vision she expressed, Gage simply said, "Looked to me like he'd consider the alternative."

"Doesn't matter. How long before he'd miss his family and resent me for making him leave them? And worse, making them suffer the loss of never knowing what happened to him."

"Maybe never. Maybe he'd just love you forever and never look back."

Valene shook her head. "Still doesn't matter. I don't want to take that chance. I find it more and more difficult to ask him to give up everything when I don't want to give up my family. At least I would still get to see you on occasion. And most of all, my family would know I was safe. Wyatt's family would be in the dark forever. I believe that even *I* would resent me, given enough time."

"You should still at least consider the glass half-full scenario, Valene."

A loud beep interrupted the difficult conversation. Gage raced to his computer. He typed madly and made an inarticulate noise, like he'd discovered something interesting.

"What is it?" Valene asked, looking over his shoulder at the screen, which displayed charts and diagrams that made no sense to her.

"I ran a system check of the cryo-pods' reboot history. Looks like one prisoner's cryo-pod *was* opened much earlier than the others during the solar flares."

"I'll bet I can guess which one."

Gage looked over his shoulder, a slight frown in place.

"Indigo Smith, right?"

He nodded. Turning to his keyboard, he tapped several keys, changing the screens into more graphs and pictures she didn't understand.

"Then there was another cryo-tube accessed a few minutes later."

"Someone else left early with him?"

"Not sure. It opened and closed. Then seventeen minutes after that a rear service hatch on the gulag ship was accessed, opened briefly and then closed."

"I can't believe no one knew about it until now."

Gage typed and more screens appeared. "No

one would have had reason to check these files if not for the solar flares opening up the cryo-pods and letting everyone escape. But you're right, someone should have noted the hatch opening and closing. Unless—"

"Unless, what?"

"One of the guards was in on it."

"Better prove that before you make any accusations."

"Oh, I will. Don't worry."

Valene pondered a moment. "You're saying that Indigo Smith already had an escape plan in place that no one would have known about until they got to the gulag, if the solar flares hadn't released everyone."

"Yes. That's my theory."

"How long was he gone before the other cryo-pods opened because of the solar flares?"

"Twenty-eight hours."

Valene thought about what she'd been doing twenty-eight hours ago when Indigo Smith had made his secret getaway. She'd been crying her eyes out alone in her room because Wyatt asked her to marry him two weeks before and she'd had to say no, again. The event crushed her spirit completely even two weeks later. She was darn near inconsolable.

"I hate to think about how long he's really been on the run and how far he's been able to travel without anyone knowing he was gone."

He likely wasn't anywhere near the other four prisoners they'd located. They would be unable to track him using the special signature Gage had discovered. Too much time had gone by. Indigo Smith could be anywhere. Maybe even out of the country. That was a horrible thought.

"That's bad." Valene didn't mean to say the words out loud, but they were the truth.

Gage nodded. "That's an understatement. A twenty-eight-hour head start is really bad, bordering on catastrophic. Alpha-Prime is going to go into full battle mode."

"What does that mean? Alpha-Prime hasn't been at war in centuries."

"They'll dust off the antique battalion war craft and send every spaceship and every single Royal Magistrate Guardsman past and present to Earth through the wormhole, sparing no excessive cost in order to get here as fast as possible to hunt him down in every corner of Earth."

"We definitely shouldn't mention it to them just yet."

"Good plan. Besides, Diesel is Fearless Leader. We'll tell him first and not over an open channel to everyone. He can decide what to do when he gets back. He can make the call to Alpha-Prime if it's warranted." Gage thought for a moment. "But maybe you should call him and get him on a private line, give him some advance warning."

Valene shook her head. "You call him." She

hated to give anyone bad news. And this was, as Gage had said, catastrophic.

Before they could battle it out over whether she would have to make that call or he would, Nova ran into Gage's lab. "Gage. Valene." She put a hand to her chest, trying to catch her breath.

"What's wrong?"

"Two things. One good and one bad, as always."

"What's the good thing?" Gage asked. Valene agreed; she wanted to hear some good news.

"The other van just pulled into the parking lot out back. Bubba and Luther have three prisoners with them, so only two remain out there."

"Great news."

"Okay, what's the bad news?" Valene asked.

"There is someone here to see Diesel."

"Who is it?" Valene asked, not wanting to hear the answer if Nova thought it was bad.

"Daphne Charlene Dumont."

Valene rolled her eyes. *Now what?*

Gage said, "Tell her he's not here, return time unknown."

Nova looked unsure. Gage insisted, "It's the truth. We don't know when Diesel and his group are coming back."

"Tell her to get lost," Valene said at the same time, her belligerent tone safely in place.

"I don't think that's a good idea." Nova's uncertainty had morphed to alarm.

"Why? What does she want?"

Nova took a deep breath. "She wouldn't say even when I purposely asked her a second time." But Nova had a look in her eye that said something was definitely amiss.

"And?"

Nova put the hand from her chest onto one hip. "Well, I may have accidentally read her mind just a little bit and realized what she's here to tell Diesel. Or at least one thing. There may be more. I don't know. I can tell you she is big trouble."

Space potatoes, that woman. "And what did you see that was on her mind?"

"Well, it involves Sheriff Wyatt Campbell and something he apparently told her." Her eyes were wide with unease. She looked at Gage, who was already totally distressed about Indigo Smith being out in the human world for more than a day longer than they'd realized.

Valene wondered when Daphne Charlene had the time to tell Wyatt anything. They'd been together all last night, since they'd picked Wyatt up at his house during their first foray into the woods, not that she planned to announce that to anyone else. They had also been together until he left to go look for the prisoners today.

"What is it?"

"I don't even want to say it out loud."

"That doesn't sound good," Gage said.

Nova already knew about Valene's relationship with Wyatt. After all, she'd helped Valene send some paperwork to HETA requesting special dispensation to marry Wyatt and move to Nocturne Falls, Georgia. Nova gave her a heated look that possibly meant she didn't want to say anything in front of Gage.

Valene turned to Gage, but he already had a plan. "Let's do this. You go upstairs and deal with Daphne Charlene for the time being, do your best to get rid of her and I'll call Diesel."

"What are you going to tell him? You don't know what Daphne Charlene is here to say."

"I'm going to tell him the good news about the other three prisoners being captured and the bad news about the star package being out for a much longer delivery than we had originally anticipated—"

"Oh, yeah. That," Valene said under her breath as Gage spoke. A single mention of her nemesis and her brain emptied of everything else.

"—and mention he has a visitor. That's all."

"Good plan."

Valene and Nova headed back upstairs. Before they reached the top step, Valene asked, "What did Wyatt tell Daphne Charlene that I don't want anyone to hear?"

"I don't know if I should tell you. Maybe I should just wait for Diesel to come back and talk to her."

"If it involves Wyatt then it involves me."

Nova looked stricken with indecision. "I was afraid you'd say that." She opened her mouth, shut it, opened it again, closed her eyes and shut her mouth a second time.

Valene was getting close to panicked. "What in the world did you see in that woman's addled brain?"

"Wyatt apparently told her that there are space aliens living in plain sight in Alienn, Arkansas at the Big Bang Truck Stop."

No!

Chapter 9

Wyatt led the group through the thickly wooded terrain for nearly seven miles. The scent of skunk wafted nearby when the wind blew. He took care to watch and avoid any possible encounters.

Diesel was right behind him, holding a specially constructed tablet that showed the map of the area and the wispy aura of the escaped prisoner they sought in real time. The signal had been fading since soon after they left the van.

"Start veering to the left in about ten yards," Diesel said in a low tone. "We're about a hundred yards away and the signal is practically nonexistent, just flashes every few seconds now. But he's stopped moving."

"Okay." Wyatt moved carefully for several yards before coming to the edge of a large clearing. He signaled for the group to stop and set his back against the trunk of a nearby oak tree just inside the perimeter. He brought his rifle up to look through the scope and search the open area beneath the nearest tree branch, dropping into his sight. On the other side of the clearing, which he realized had an eight-foot-wide stream running through the center, Wyatt spotted his quarry seated on a large rock on the opposite bank.

"Got him," Wyatt said. The alien had obviously crossed the water and had quite possibly stopped for a nice swim, as his head, furry chest and hairy arms were as sodden as the gray prison pants he wore.

Diesel, binoculars in hand, moved next to Wyatt. He let out a grunt of satisfaction when he saw the escapee.

"Can you make that shot from here?"

Does a bear poop in the woods? The phrase was on the tip of Wyatt's tongue. He managed not to say it out loud, but only barely.

Instead, he said, "Easy."

"Do it."

Wyatt dropped his head, looked through the scope, took aim, squeezed the trigger and hit the hairy alien beast in the chest, dead center. The alien fell backward against the rock, flattening out with arms and legs stretched wide.

By the time they all made their way across the clearing and through the water, the alien was sitting up, glassy stare in place, waiting for them to command him.

"Are you alone?" Diesel asked Mr. Hairy and Wet.

The alien nodded.

"Did you see any other escaped prisoners out here in the trees?"

The alien shook his head.

Diesel looked over at Cam. "Take a group and look around the area just to be sure."

Cam took off with a group of five others, but came back several minutes later shaking his head. "There aren't any tracks or broken branches or any signs anyone else was with him," Cam said.

They put restraints on the alien prisoner and led him back through the woods to the van. The pungent scent of the alien, who'd obviously tangled with a skunk or two during his escape, made Wyatt's eyes water. He wished they *could* strap him on the roof under a tarp instead of putting him in the van with the rest of them for the return to the truck stop.

Breathing through his mouth, Wyatt contemplated how long it would take him to walk back to Alienn if he didn't ride in the van with the overpowering stench.

Before the alien was stuffed in the far back row of the van, Cam pulled a small aerosol can out of the glove compartment and sprayed the contents all over the calm, shackled alien, head to toe, back, front and sides, immediately neutralizing the gag-worthy stench.

"What is that amazing stuff and how can I get a fifty-five-gallon drum of it?" Wyatt asked.

Cam gave him a tight smile. "This is alien

technology. Unfortunately, it is unavailable for distribution to humans."

"Right." Wyatt nodded. "That's too bad. You could make a zillion dollars selling that stuff, maybe more."

One of his father's large dogs got sprayed by a skunk the winter before. They had tried everything to get the smell out of Mojo's thick fur including a tub of tomato juice, a tub of vinegar and some concoction of peroxide and lavender, none of which had taken all of the skunk scent completely out. It might have been a factor that Mojo really hated baths and was highly resistant to taking them, especially by the third time they tried to de-skunk scent him by dunking the big goofy dog into yet another tub of smelly liquid.

The radio at Diesel's hip crackled to life with a pre-established code as one short and one long press on the push to talk button signaled someone wanted to communicate.

Diesel answered. "Base Station, this is the NW team. What's up? Over."

"Where are you?" It was Gage's voice not Valene's.

"Good news, Base Station. We are about to transport one package back home in the van."

"Copy that, one package. The NE team just returned with three packages."

Around Wyatt and Diesel, the volunteers perked up. Even Cam's eyebrows raised with the question on everyone's mind: Was Indigo Smith one of the three?

"Let me guess—none of them are the celebrity package we wanted to ensure was found."

"Copy that. The *celebrity* package is still at large. I also have additional and rather interesting information regarding that special package. What is your ETA?"

"Estimated time of arrival is less than thirty minutes. What's interesting about the additional information?"

"The package has been out for delivery much longer than originally believed."

"Oh?" Diesel's head dropped, face pointing to the ground when he asked grimly, "How long?"

"Twenty-eight hours longer than the package you have in your possession now."

"That's bad." Wyatt uttered those words in a quiet tone, and Diesel nodded.

"Copy that. It is the consensus here, as well."

Wyatt said, "That truly sucks because with a twenty-eight-hour head start, he could be anywhere by now. Out of Arkansas, certainly, but maybe even out of the country." The entire group had gone from perky to pessimistic in seconds and looked shaken.

Diesel said, "I hate to ask, but is there anything else I need to know?"

Gage came back on the line. "Well, sort of."

Diesel's head tilted toward the sky. His eyes rolled when he asked, "What else is there?"

"Um…you have a…a visitor waiting to speak to you upon your return."

"Tell whoever it is that I'm unavailable."

"I'll try. But I don't know if that's a good idea."

"I do. I don't have time for a confab with anyone. This new complication with our celebrity package rules all. We'll see you in thirty minutes or less. NW team out."

"Copy that. Base Station out."

Wyatt missed hearing Valene's voice and wondered why she hadn't made the call. Was she dealing with the person waiting to see Diesel, who was now unavailable?

He didn't quite understand why the Indigo Smith prisoner had been gone longer than the recently de-skunked alien.

Not that he wanted any dangerous alien criminals roaming the area, but he also hoped that with still one prisoner left to find, he'd be allowed to keep his memories for the time being. Then again, maybe only one escapee left to catch meant his time with Valene would shortly come to an end. They already had another sharpshooter on the other team, the pale alien named Luther. Maybe Wyatt's services would no longer be required. That thought deflated him until a worse one occurred.

Would they warn him or just blast him and let him wander back into his life with a year of memories gone? Which would be worse? He wasn't sure.

Wyatt kept an eye out for Cam or anyone else putting a hand on the Defender thing strapped to all of their belts. Maybe he'd be allowed one last-ditch effort to promise to love, honor and cherish their only sister. Or perhaps not. She mentioned not wanting to leave her family. Her brothers likely felt the same. Either way, he planned to keep his guard up for the trip back to Alienn and any possible Defender blasts to his person.

After secretly spending last night with Valene, he wasn't certain what his future held. Would Valene share that? She'd been rather adamant that their night together should remain a confidential matter between just the two of them. They'd discussed it this morning.

Then again, they all worried he might give away their big *space aliens living in plain sight* secret, so he understood the need for a memory wipe in his future, whether they warned him about it in advance or not. But he hoped for at least a chance to speak to Valene one last time, if that was the way it had to be.

Wyatt loved Valene. It was as simple as that. So when the time came, if they did warn him about the needed memory wipe, he planned to tell them he would marry Valene. He would go to their planet two galaxies away and live there with her for the rest of his life, even if it meant his family would never know what happened to him. It would be difficult, but he was determined.

He'd barely made his way through two weeks without her when they'd broken up.

Wyatt's life without Valene was no way to live.

"What?!" Valene's stomach felt like it dropped to the floor. She shook her head. She refused to believe it. Wyatt would never tell their alien secret. Never. She wanted to crush and destroy anyone who could dare repeat such a despicable story.

Nova opened her mouth to repeat the worst imaginable situation in an Alpha's world. A human, and especially Daphne Charlene, discovering their secret. Valene put her forefinger up to Nova's lips to keep her from repeating such a wicked, vile falsehood.

"No. Don't ever say that again. It is a lie. She's lying."

Nova pulled Valene's finger away. "It was in Daphne Charlene's mind, Valene. She doesn't know I heard her thoughts. At least you are forewarned. I'll admit I was pretty surprised because I always thought of Wyatt as a standup, honorable guy." They continued up the stairs until they reached the hallway near the upstairs back offices.

Valene stopped in the middle of the hallway that led to the convenience store. "He *is* a standup honorable guy." *Besides, when could he have told that woman anything?*

Nova put her hands up. "I've never doubted that before, but you should also know that I saw more and it's worse."

"More? Worse? I don't believe it! I am already well over my capacity for horrific news."

"Well, I believe you'll think it's worse."

"Are we going to do good news, bad news again? Because I'm sick to death of that game."

Nova slumped. "Her knowing that information is a big problem for all of us, Valene. I like Earth, too, just like all of us living here do. But this is dang near cataclysmic in the realm of bad news."

Valene straightened, took a breath and tried to still her wildly stricken nerves. "Okay. I know. You're right. What is the worse news?"

"Inside her mind I also saw a half-dressed version of Wyatt wearing sleep pants so low that I could see his appendix scar. I'm not certain if that means the obvious, but it's probably best for you to know before meeting up with Daphne Charlene."

Valene's mouth dropped open yet again. She hadn't expected any worse news about Wyatt. "No, that can't be true."

"I'm so sorry, Valene. I didn't mean to see it. Well, I did of course because I willfully read her mind, but I didn't mean to see such bad news for you. I wouldn't have believed it if she'd just told me, but in her mind, she's definitely seen Wyatt half-dressed."

She stared at Nova, eyes widening in vivid horror. Her head moved back and forth, the scream she wanted to release caught in her throat.

Valene had seen that scar herself for the very first time last night. She had run her fingertip over the surface, asking how old he'd been when he got it. How could Daphne Charlene possibly know about it, unless she'd also been with Wyatt? *No. No. Please don't let that be true.*

Nova had the good sense to grab Valene and ease her gently into a row of visitor seats. Her legs gave out just as she plopped onto her butt in the molded plastic chair in the hallway leading to the Fearless Leader's office.

She rocked back and forth, her arms wrapped around her middle, feeling betrayed like never before. The tears that had threatened to spill let loose, streaming down her face as she let go the agonized sobs that would not be stopped.

Nova sat down next to her, put a comforting arm around Valene's shoulders and squeezed her as the misery leaked out.

When she finally settled, Nova said, "Listen, I was shocked at first, too. So I thought about it on my way down to the basement. It occurs to me that there are lots of ways that woman could know about Wyatt's scar."

"Like how?"

"Maybe she knows someone who was a nurse during his procedure. Maybe a friend of Wyatt's mother told someone and Daphne Charlene got the information by accident."

Valene sniffed. She wanted so much to believe that Wyatt would never betray her and especially not with the likes of Daphne Charlene.

Every time he'd spoken of *that woman* it was with a certain contempt in his tone. He truly didn't seem to like her. Something occurred to Valene.

"Tell me, Nova. What did Wyatt's scar look like?"

Nova's eyes widened. "Well, I only got a quick look, you understand."

"I know, but tell me what you remember."

"Wyatt obviously works out. He has very nice abs."

"Yes. He does. What else? Tell me about the appendix scar." Valene was more interested in the description. Wyatt's scar was unique. Not the clean-lined, flat scar it might have been, but jagged with raised, angry dark pink tissue due to the unusual nature of its removal.

Wyatt told her he'd gotten his rather ugly scar because an EMT had done emergency surgery on him when he was nine years old and in an ambulance on the way to the hospital. The only doctor on staff had been knocked unconscious by a quarrelsome, loudmouthed ER patient, and the standby doctor was too far away to get to Wyatt's surgery in a timely manner.

Afraid Wyatt might die if the appendix ruptured

en route, the standby doctor talked the EMT through the procedure as the ambulance raced across town to the hospital. His appendix had partially burst as it was being removed during the rough ride, but he and his parents had been told he only survived because it was taken out so quickly. He very likely would not have made it to the hospital in time had they waited.

"The scar is sort of lightning shaped."

What? "Do you mean it's jagged?"

"Yes. Right. Jagged. And it has pink, raised tissue." Nova made a face. "It kind of looks like they used a butter knife to do the surgery as I think about it."

Valene's mouth trembled. So, it was true. Daphne Charlene must have seen the scar. Tears splashed onto her cheeks as the disturbing truth peeked through.

Nova took her by the shoulders and shook her gently. "Listen to me, Valene. Don't let her get into your head. If Daphne Charlene knows or says something, that doesn't mean the obvious."

"What do you mean? If she has *that* vision in her head, then she's seen him in his pajamas. Trust me, I know that firsthand."

Nova looked up as if searching her memory for a plausible explanation. "I know—what if she looked in his window?"

Valene grunted. "Doubtful."

"Why?"

"Wyatt keeps all his windows shut, locked and the bedrooms have blackout curtains."

"Oh, so he doesn't ever walk around the rest of his house in pajama pants? I don't buy it. And I also don't believe Wyatt cares one whit about her. He loves you. I heard he said it out loud this morning in front of your brothers."

Valene huffed. "Word sure does travel fast."

"There are not many secrets in a small town, Valene, as you well know. Besides," Nova said, lifting her hand, "the ring on your finger says something about Wyatt and his intentions, don't you think?"

Valene gazed at the beautiful ring, allowing Nova's words to seep inside. "Wait a minute. Weren't you the one questioning his honor when we started this conversation?"

Nova sighed. "Well, I've changed my mind. I'm allowed to do that because I'm a woman of a certain age. An age, mind you, that the details of which will never be revealed. Given the choice between Wyatt or Daphne Charlene, I'm putting my money on Wyatt."

Valene decided to put her money on Wyatt, too. She stood up and Nova stood with her. "What are you going to do?"

"I'm going to go talk to Daphne Charlene."

Nova looked suddenly wary. "What will you say to her, or rather, do to her?"

"Nothing permanent."

Nova grabbed her arm. "What does that mean?"

"I'm kidding. I'll just go see what she wants to talk to Diesel about. If it's what you read in her mind then I'll lure her back here and shoot her with a Defender."

"What if she doesn't tell you?"

Valene shrugged. "Same thing."

Nova reached out to grab her again, but Valene was faster, staying out of reach. "Don't worry, Nova. I won't do anything rash." *Probably.*

Valene walked slowly into the convenience store. She passed an attractive man who was looking at all of the Maxwell the Martian merchandise and seemed a bit frantic.

"Excuse me," he said before she got too far away.

She turned back and stared at the stranger. He was fairly tall with straight, icy-blond hair and a really engaging smile. She moved toward him without thinking.

"Yes?"

"You work here, right?"

She looked down to see if she was wearing her name badge, but she wasn't. "How do you know that?"

His eyes narrowed. He turned and pointed to the door she'd just passed through. "You just walked out of the employees only door. I took a chance."

Valene nodded. "Right. Well, I'm not on duty, but I'll do my best to help you, if I can."

"Great. I'm looking for a special gift for my niece. She's ten and she loves all things outer space. I thought she'd get a kick out of something here. I'm just not sure what a ten-year-old girl would like. Do you think you could help me out?"

"Sure." Valene moved over to the rack of Maxwell the Martian doll merchandise and selected a medium-sized stuffed Maxwell, handing it to the man. "I was crazy for stuffed animals when I was ten. This one is the perfect size."

He took the offered Maxwell, smiled and put his hand on her shoulder, squeezing gently. "Thank you very much for helping me." His voice sounded oddly low and seductive. "Could I buy you a cup of cheap truck stop coffee to pay you back?" He grinned, showing off a row of straight white teeth any movie star would covet.

Valene considered his proposal to have coffee. It was really nice of him to offer when she hadn't done much. Did she have time? She glanced around, trying to remember why she was up here in the truck stop in the first place.

Daphne Charlene loitered by the front cash register, throwing ice-cold water on her impromptu coffee date. Wyatt's face came into her mind and she shook off any idea of having coffee with a handsome stranger. "Not necessary. But thank you for your kindness."

The man took his hand from her shoulder, smiled shyly and nodded. "Well, thanks anyway."

Valene mentally shook off whatever *that* was and made her way toward Daphne Charlene. Before she got halfway there, Diesel appeared out of nowhere. He strode up to Daphne Charlene and asked, "I understand you were looking for me?"

Daphne Charlene looked very perturbed. "What took you so long? I've been waiting for almost twenty-five minutes."

"Well, I'm a busy man. In fact, you only have two minutes to tell me whatever is on your mind, then I have other things to attend to."

Valene moved closer, wondering how Diesel got to the truck stop so fast. Hadn't he been thirty minutes away when she came upstairs? How long had she cried on Nova's shoulder about Wyatt and Daphne Charlene's intimate knowledge about his appendix scar?

"I have some information about Sheriff Wyatt Campbell."

"Don't believe anything she says, Diesel," Valene said, joining their conversation.

Diesel frowned at Valene and looked over her shoulder at the charming man she'd helped, who was now purchasing the stuffed Maxwell the Martian she'd helped select for his ten-year-old niece.

The man waved at her and Valene grinned and waved back.

Daphne Charlene said casually, "I just thought you should know that Wyatt told me something very interesting about your little truck stop operation last night when we were together."

Valene straightened like she'd been hit by a bolt of lightning. "You were not with him last night."

"How do you know?"

"Because I was."

"You weren't with him the whole night, were you?" Daphne Charlene looked smug.

"Yes. In fact, I was. He was right beside me in his king-sized bed. All night long." Valene turned to Diesel and realized what she'd just admitted.

Diesel's eyebrows lifted, but he remained silent.

Daphne Charlene smiled like a cat with canary feathers poking out of its mouth. "Well, I was with him in his kitchen for over thirty minutes very late last night. I didn't see you there. Then again, we didn't take the time to go all the way to the bedroom. Right after our intimacy, though, he told me the most interesting story about aliens living in plain sight at this very truck stop." She grinned as if she'd won some sort of trophy for whatever *intimacy* they'd shared and ensuring Valene knew about it.

She started to make a vulgar remark, but then something unnerving from the night before materialized in her mind.

Valene froze in place as an elusive memory drifted up from her dreamy memories of the night spent with the man she loved beyond reason. She'd woken in Wyatt's bed all alone. She reached an arm out to feel for him, but didn't find him there and the space where he'd been was cold.

When she'd forced her lids open, she'd seen three twenty-three in red numbers on the digital bedside clock. She sat up and called out Wyatt's name in the darkness. Twice. He'd strolled in a few moments later, climbed into bed and snuggled up to her, mumbling something about the barking dogs next door.

"You're lying." Valene gave the other woman her best death stare, but Daphne Charlene wasn't cowed.

She turned to Diesel. "I have something to tell you. However, I don't think your sister should listen in. Don't want to hurt her *delicate* feelings."

"Diesel, don't listen to her. She's a liar."

Valene couldn't read Diesel's expression. He put a hand on her shoulder and said, "Let me handle this. Cam wants to talk to you in his office."

"Cam? Why?"

"Don't know. Why don't you go see him and find out?" Diesel's tone was the Fearless Leader one that brooked no nonsense.

Valene huffed. "You're just trying to get rid of me."

Diesel gave her a half smile and squeezed her shoulder. "Go on now."

Daphne Charlene cast her a triumphant look, but Valene knew the lying woman was about to be coaxed through the *Employees Only* hallway, back to Diesel's office and blasted with a Defender no matter what lies she told.

She gave Daphne Charlene a rather smug look in return and shuffled slowly toward the back. She looked over her shoulder twice to see Diesel watching until she was gone before engaging Daphne Charlene in conversation.

Once she made it downstairs, Valene headed for Cam's office. She knocked and Wyatt answered. He was all alone in the room.

"Where's Cam?"

"He left me alone so we could chat." Valene's spirits lifted at the idea of alone time with Wyatt. She moved closer for a hug until his expression stopped her dead in her tracks.

"What's wrong?"

"A couple of things. First off, who was that blond guy you were laughing and carrying on with upstairs for so long?"

Valene shrugged. "I don't know, some customer looking for a gift for his niece. Besides, I didn't talk to him that long. I don't remember carrying on with him." Why was Wyatt acting jealous? She was the one who'd had to deal with Daphne Charlene.

"I guess it depends on your definition. Seemed like quite a bit of time to me." Wyatt didn't look very happy about her talking to anyone. "Plus, he had his hand on your shoulder. Kind of extra familiar, if you ask me."

"I didn't ask." Valene didn't mean to be so short

with him, but another question floated to the surface. "How did you guys get here so fast?" She looked at the clock on Cam's wall and saw it was half an hour later than she thought. "Is that the right time?"

Wyatt glanced at the clock and nodded.

Valene remembered what Nova had told her when she read Daphne Charlene's thoughts. Not to mention her bombshell information regarding aliens hiding in plain sight at the truck shop.

"Were you with Daphne Charlene last night?"

He gave her a sharp look. "No. I was with you."

"But in the middle of the night I woke up and you were gone."

"I heard the dogs barking again so I went out back to take a look." He shrugged.

"Your side of the bed was cold when I felt the sheets. You must have been taking a really long look."

Wyatt looked skyward and sighed. "I might have been thinking about our future. I might have sat in the kitchen at my table and pondered living with you…elsewhere."

"Daphne Charlene says she was with you in your kitchen late last night."

He frowned. "And you believed her?"

Valene stared at him. "She also said you told her about space aliens living in plain sight at the Big Bang Truck Stop. How could she know that if you didn't tell her?"

Wyatt's eyes widened, but he didn't have time to say anything before the door opened and Cam stepped in, Defender in hand.

Before Valene could do anything, Cam shot Wyatt and he crumpled to the floor, unconscious.

"Why did you do that?" Valene said, dropping down to see if Wyatt was okay.

"Because Daphne Charlene just ratted him out to Diesel. Said Wyatt told her about our big secret during pillow talk."

"She's lying, Wyatt would never divulge that secret, with or without a pillow." Hadn't she just accused Wyatt of that very thing? She was a hypocrite.

"All right then, tell me this—how else could she know?"

Valene opened her mouth to defend Wyatt, but nothing came out. The memories from the night before raced in to fill her head with a variety of what-if scenarios and none of them cleared Wyatt.

Who else had recently been told about aliens living in plain sight at the truck stop?

No one that Valene could name. Why would Wyatt tell Daphne Charlene anything about that unless they were together? Valene couldn't think of a single situation to make that deplorable information work.

Chapter 10

Wyatt woke up in Gage's lab again, only this time he was strapped down and couldn't move. His last memory was trying to convince Valene that Daphne Charlene was not a viable candidate for his affections even if his memory was erased. And seeing the surveillance tape Gage watched of Valene with some customer in the convenience store.

Nova also watched the tape, her awe-filled expression and subsequent blush when Wyatt walked in on the tape made him wonder how long Valene had been chatting, or rather flirting, with the blond guy before they arrived back with the hairy, un-skunk-scented alien.

Cam directed Wyatt to his office and told him he'd send Valene in so they could have a chat. When Valene finally arrived, they'd only spoken for a few moments. He hadn't yet convinced her that Daphne Charlene was lying about meeting with him in the middle of the night. Then he blacked out and woke up here.

"Hello. Hey!" he called out, hoping he wasn't alone. Scenes from every alien horror movie he'd ever seen slid uneasily into his mind before Gage stepped into view.

"Hey, Wyatt. How do you feel?"

"Trapped."

"Oh, yeah. Sorry for the straps. Cam made me do it for security." Gage seemed genuinely uncomfortable, but he also didn't attempt to remove the bands tying Wyatt down.

"Why? What is going on here?"

"It's because of what Daphne Charlene said you told her. You know, about us being aliens and all. That's pretty much rule number one around here. Don't tell any humans where we're from."

Wyatt paused. "I swear that I didn't tell her anything. I don't like her. I would never tell her."

Gage nodded. He seemed to believe Wyatt, but before he could comment, Cam strolled in.

"Wyatt," he said.

"You shot me with a Defender."

"I did."

"Why?"

"Daphne Charlene says you two have an intimate relationship and that during pillow talk you mentioned space aliens living in plain sight at the Big Bang Truck Stop. We can't have that information spreading around town. You understand."

Wyatt felt his own eyes widen. "I swear to you on all I hold dear that I never told her anything.

Trust me, there was never any pillow talk between us."

"Right. That's because last night you were with Valene instead."

Relieved, Wyatt quickly said, "Yes. Yes, I was."

"All night?"

"Yes!" he said emphatically, until Wyatt realized what he'd just revealed to one of Valene's six older brothers. *So dumb.* "Well...yes. We were together," he admitted. After a long, uncomfortable staring contest, he added, "The thing is, I love Valene. I want to marry her. I have for quite a while now."

"That's all fine and good, but the problem is, how can Daphne Charlene Dumont know about our big secret unless it came from you?"

"I don't know. But I swear to you I didn't tell her anything."

Cam loosened the straps until he was free. "I want to believe you."

Wyatt sat up and got off the table. "But you don't."

"Is it possible that you were drugged or somehow induced to tell her against your will?"

"All I can say is that's what it would take to get that specific information out of me. I wouldn't willingly tell anyone and especially not Daphne Charlene. Besides, as loath as I am to admit this to you, Valene and I were together at my house all night long. Ask her."

"I have. Given what I know, it's possible you

just bought yourself a one-way ticket to a new rest-of-your-life on Alpha-Prime."

Wyatt shrugged. "I'm okay with that."

"Are you? What if Valene doesn't go with you?"

"What? Why wouldn't she?"

"Daphne Charlene has made a compelling case for pillow talk with you. Valene's feelings were hurt in the process. I will delay discussion of the 'night' you spent together until after this current catastrophe is resolved."

"Where is she?"

"Daphne Charlene?"

"No! Valene."

"Diesel sent her home. A rare alien council meeting is about to take place to talk about Daphne Charlene being a possible tattletale along with the dispiriting news about Indigo Smith likely hiding in another country after being gone for over a day longer than we suspected.

"I'm afraid that there are only two scenarios in your case. Either you will be shackled and sent to Alpha-Prime or, more likely, your memory will be erased."

Wyatt thought about it for a few moments. "My memory will be erased to before you told me about the Big Bang Truck Stop?"

Cam didn't answer right away. "That's one scenario. But I'm afraid the more popular plan is to take your memories all the way back to before you and Valene became a secret couple."

"How will that work? There are other humans that know we're together. Hunter Valero, to just name one. And, of course, my family."

Cam shrugged. "The process looks into the mind and identifies any possible points of contact and an analysis will suggest possible action for each one. They'll be dealt with on a case-by-case basis. This is not our first rodeo."

Wyatt nodded, but his mind was zipping here and there at a hundred miles an hour trying to figure out how Daphne Charlene could have found out anything. Nothing came to mind. How in the world could he convince anyone he didn't tattle? Again, nothing came to mind.

"I can see into your mind, Wyatt," Cam said all of a sudden. He seemed less hostile, if that were possible.

"What do you see?"

"You believe you didn't tell anyone about us. Therefore, I'll give you the benefit of the doubt, which I probably would have anyway."

Wyatt took small comfort that at least Cam believed him, to a degree. Would Valene? What would he say to her if he was granted the opportunity before his memories were blasted away? He was very worried about Valene being hurt by what Daphne Charlene said. He wouldn't feel better until he could look her in the eyes, hold her hand and tell her in person that he wasn't responsible.

Wyatt nodded. "Can I ask a favor?"

"Sure."

"Is there any way I could talk to Valene before any drastic measures are taken with me regarding my pending memory loss?"

"I'll see what I can do, but no promises."

Perhaps his best bet was convincing Valene to move to Alpha-Prime with him. Would she consider that or believe that he'd spent *intimate* time with Daphne Charlene?

And if he couldn't convince Valene he'd been true, maybe it would be best if a year's worth of memories *were* deleted. It was the only way he could think of not to be miserable for the rest of his natural life.

Valene had been summarily dismissed. She wanted to attend the special council meeting. Diesel decided differently and sent her home. She didn't want to go home to pace and brood. She wanted to talk to Wyatt and discover the truth, but likely Diesel or one of her annoying brothers would keep her from that until they determined if he'd outed them. Deep down, Valene believed he couldn't possibly have done it, but she wouldn't know for certain until she looked him in the eyes, held his hand and asked.

Instead, she went to drown her sorrows at the

Cosmos Café using giant Mason jar glasses full of sweet tea. She slurped the last bit of her second glass through a straw and signaled for another.

Aunt Dixie put the third large glass on the table and said, "After this, I'm cutting you off."

"Why? It's sweet tea not whiskey."

"For your own good. You don't want to spend the rest of the night in the bathroom peeing, do you?"

"Whatever."

Her aunt crossed her arms and let out a distasteful harrumph. "Is this a pity party for one or may I join you?"

"It's just for one." She didn't want company or any advice.

"Too bad." Aunt Dixie seated herself across the booth and put a hand on Valene's. "Tell me what happened."

Valene resisted for about two seconds, but knew her aunt was like a bulldog on a discovery mission and would not stop hounding her until she gave in and spilled all. Valene gave her the quick version in whispers so none of the few other patrons would hear how she'd spent the night with Wyatt, and about Daphne Charlene's catastrophic gossip that she supposedly learned from Wyatt during intimate pillow talk in the kitchen last night.

She finished with Nova's mind reading vision of Wyatt in his pajamas showing his appendix scar, giving some credibility to Daphne Charlene's version of events.

"Daphne Charlene is a big, fat liar." Aunt Dixie was not one to sugarcoat things.

"Maybe so, but how does she know our big secret and where did she see Wyatt in his pajama pants?"

Aunt Dixie chewed over that in silence. All of a sudden, her eyes lit up as if some brilliant piece of information had just entered her head. "Didn't you tell me once that Wyatt was born up north somewhere and only came to Arkansas when he was a little kid?"

Valene was regretting telling Dixie Lou Grey anything. "Yes. He was born in Minnesota, near Duluth, I think, but it doesn't matter. He's been here since he was, like, three years old. Besides, what difference does that make?"

"I'm not sure yet." Aunt Dixie had that look that said the wheels were spinning like mad inside her head. That was not good.

"Listen, I appreciate you wanting to help—"

"I remember something special about a place in Minnesota. Where did I see that?" She seemed to mumble the second question to herself.

"What does Minnesota have to do with anything?" Valene asked.

A wide grin shaped Aunt Dixie's mouth with what looked like a hearty dollop of resolve and she said, "I don't know yet, but I'm on the case."

Oh no. What case? "What do you mean by that, Aunt Dixie?"

Aunt Dixie stopped mumbling and turned a loving look on Valene. "It means that I think you and Wyatt should be together, but I'd hate for you to move away to Alpha-Prime. So I'll do whatever I can to ensure that you get a happily ever after with your guy *and* stay in Alienn. Don't you worry about a thing." She patted Valene's hand and exited the booth with a spring in her step.

Valene smiled inwardly for the first time since being ordered away from the truck stop. Aunt Dixie was a wily hoot of an old woman, but Valene didn't doubt she'd give it her all. Then again, Valene wasn't foolish enough to believe she'd get to have her happily ever after in this case, no matter what crazy idea her aunt came up with.

Wyatt was a human. And whether he was born in Arkansas or Minnesota, nothing was going to change that fact.

"Hey, fancy meeting you here," said a familiar voice.

She was surprised into asking, "What are *you* doing here?"

"Well, now, that's a long story."

Valene gestured to the seat Aunt Dixie had vacated and said, "Well, have a seat, I've got time." She took a deep sip of her third glass of sweet tea, ready to listen to a long story. Maybe it would take her mind off her troubles.

✦

Dixie Lou Grey had never been a shrinking flower. Chasing down a way for her favorite niece to remain on Earth with Skeeter Bite Sheriff Wyatt Campbell, her true love and a human, had turned into quite a daunting task. The only way she could think of for Wyatt to be allowed into their family was if he didn't have any family of his own. But he had a large, close, happy family and, bless her heart, Valene didn't want to hurt them by taking Wyatt away from them forever.

Dixie Lou would have to think of something else. She pondered and paced and thought and thought. Out of the blue, a long shot of an idea came to her in the form of the Lost Colony Legend. She hadn't thought about it since Diesel's wedding.

When Juliana Masters, Diesel's wife, had first come to Alienn, she didn't have anyone except Miss Penny looking out for her. At the time, although Dixie Lou had never voiced it, the thought occurred to her that if Juliana hadn't been a distant ancestor of a previously failed Alpha-Prime colony project to live on Earth, maybe they could have faked her death and let her recreate herself as an Alpha. But that extreme idea hadn't been needed and Dixie Lou tucked it away for possible use at a later date.

With Wyatt's big family, faking his death was out of the question. She pondered, paced and thought some more. There had to be a way to make this romance work out.

All this information about the past teased her long-held interest in the Alpha-Prime Lost Colony project that had brought Miss Penny to Earth long ago and eventually Juliana and both of them to Alienn. Once upon a time, Dixie had sought out and clipped every newspaper article she could find that whispered anything about aliens living on Earth. She had several scrapbooks on Roswell, New Mexico alone.

But her favorite alien invading Earth stories were from less well-known places.

The knowledge that Wyatt's family had moved here many years ago from Minnesota had piqued her memory. She had once clipped an article or two from a place in Minnesota that might have aliens or maybe mind readers or something. Anyway, Alpha-Prime had sent an agent to check it out and Dixie Lou was certain she'd clipped an article or two about it.

Dixie Lou went straight to the narrow stairwell leading up to her attic. She needed to look up some history in her scrapbooks. It had been a long time since she'd looked at them.

She opened the door at the top step and sneezed twice as dust swirled around her. Dixie vowed to bring her dust buster with her next time. Searching the hot, humid, close space, she spied an old wooden sea trunk she'd gotten for a steal at an estate sale fifty years ago and raised the unlocked lid.

Inside was a veritable treasure trove of history in the form of carefully preserved scrapbooks. They covered decades. When she'd been younger and after her own family had gone, she had come to Earth to start over.

Valene had been a baby then. Dixie Lou had a whole bunch of photo scrapbooks in her little den downstairs of the seven kids from when they were little to now.

Dixie Lou pulled the scrapbooks out one by one until she got to the very first few memory books, ones she'd created upon her arrival on Earth. She unsealed the second book labeled by dates and flipped through history as old memories of times gone by filled her mind, making her wistful for friends long gone.

She became so steeped in history she almost forgot why she'd cracked the scrapbook open. Then she found the three articles she'd been looking for.

The first was from the Alpha-Prime *Earthly Gazette*, a monthly circular from back home that listed stories about commerce between the colony on Earth and Alpha-Prime. The article was about an agent sent by the Royal Magistrate Guard Academy to a place called Superstition, Minnesota to investigate after a few stories filtered back to Alpha-Prime about people there who *supposedly* could read minds.

The agent was in Minnesota for a few weeks to search out and either prove or disprove any alien, especially any Alpha, mind-reading activity. The fledgling agent was female, not unusual for Alpha-Prime, but more so for Earth in that time period. The first article was short, simply announcing her assignment and a brief description of the agent, Constance Brickwood. It included a black-and-white photo of a shorter than average, rather willowy Alpha. Constance had a serious and rather hollow look for someone as young as she was. Dixie Lou remembered thinking when she clipped the article that the agent had the expression of someone who was haunted.

The second article was about the report she sent back to the powers in the Alpha-Prime Royal Magistrate Guard a month later. Constance was of the opinion that while there were a greater than average amount of psychic businesses and the town had been named to help generate even more interest in palmistry and the like, she could find no Alpha influence in the area. Her conclusion: Humans in pursuit of the paranormal were responsible and simply trying to make a living by entertaining other earthlings.

A couple of weeks later, a third, very short, article reported the tragic loss of Constance in an accident that claimed her life before she left Earth.

She had been interred in a small church cemetery in Superstition, Minnesota, as poor Constance had no remaining family left back on Alpha-Prime.

Dixie Lou always thought that to be unusual.

Even now, she wondered why the authorities on Alpha-Prime hadn't insisted on bringing Constance back home for interment. She looked through a few more of her scrapbooks, but didn't see any other references to Constance Brickwood, Superstition or any Alpha aliens living there.

After sitting cross-legged for too long, Dixie Lou stood up, stretched and did several squats to get the blood back into her legs. She scooped up the scrapbook with the three Superstition stories inside. She carefully packed her other precious scrapbooks back in the old bargain sea trunk and went downstairs.

She'd look on the computer machine to find out any further information. The computer had all sorts of information available. It had almost everything. If you knew what you were looking for, anyway.

Before she made it to her den, there was a knock at the door.

She opened it to see her very best friend, Miss Penny. "What's cookin'?" Dixie Lou asked her friend, like she always did.

Miss Penny cackled and answered, "Not my goose, at least not today." Just like *she* always did.

Dixie Lou opened the door wide. "Come on in, Miss Penny. I'm on a mission. It's a secret one, so keep it under your hat."

"Ooh. Sounds exciting. Can I help you on this secret mission? You know I can be trusted not to gossip."

"Course you can. I'd love some help. This might be our greatest adventure yet."

"Where are we going?"

"Minnesota."

"Sounds perfect. I've never been that way before. I'd love to go. How are we getting up there?"

Dixie Lou put a finger to her cheek. "I'm not quite sure yet. But we'll think of something."

"What do we do first?"

"I need to do a bit of research in the computer machine and then we'll make our plans."

"That sounds fine."

Dixie Lou thought back to her chat with Valene at the Cosmos Café, remembering the wistful, unhappy look on her niece's face because she couldn't marry the man she loved. Dixie Lou didn't know if this plan of hers would result in anything helpful, but it was worth a try, to her mind.

Once she and Miss Penny had prepared and eaten a little snack, they went into her small den and turned the computer on.

Her nephews had all taken turns helping her try to navigate the internet highway, but sweet Valene had been the most patient and the most helpful. She had written various instructions down so Dixie Lou could go back and follow them for whatever she needed to do.

She found the local online paper in Superstition, the *Superstition Examiner*. The town was about seventy miles north of Duluth. After reading only a few things, Dixie Lou looked at Miss Penny and said, "Superstition, Minnesota is very suspicious."

"Why do you say that?"

"Fifty years ago, an Alpha agent was sent to ensure there were no mind-reading Alpha aliens there. But even today they have quite a booming year-round business in the trade."

Miss Penny shrugged. "Maybe they are human mind readers."

"I don't know about that. It sounds fishy to me," Dixie Lou said, scrolling through the latest news articles for the area.

"Why do you say that? I've heard of lots of human psychics. They even have television shows sometimes."

Dixie Lou scrolled past a picture and then scrolled up to look at it again.

Her mouth dropped open.

"What's wrong with you? Close your mouth, Dixie Lou," Miss Penny said. She leaned in to see what Dixie Lou was staring at. It was a picture of an older woman with an older man, maybe her husband. They sat in rocking chairs on a porch, hands clasped sweetly together.

"That's...that's..." Dixie Lou was flabbergasted.

"Who? Who is it?"

"Constance Brickwood."

"Never heard of her," Miss Penny said, sitting back in her chair.

Dixie Lou stood up and started pacing. If

Constance Brickwood hadn't died and been buried, why had she stayed in Superstition instead of going back to Alpha-Prime fifty years ago? The picture looked exactly like her, only a bit older. Alpha genes were awesome.

She snapped her fingers. "We need wheels."

"Wheels?" Miss Penny also stood up.

"Yes. You know, transportation."

"Where are we going?"

"Superstition, Minnesota. We're going to visit a woman who's supposedly been dead for fifty years."

Diesel took a deep breath and wondered what in the space potato farm would happen next.

He'd managed to lure Daphne Charlene into his office and give her a blast with the Defender. Then he'd handed the unconscious woman off to Gage and called an emergency meeting to discuss the problem.

He entered the conference room full of people braced for nothing less than a call-to-arms about handling a possible earthling discovery of their big secret on top of the recent news that the infamous Indigo Smith was at large somewhere on Earth. It was a banner day for bad news.

He hoped someone had a brilliant idea about what they should do, besides his current favorite nightmare scenario of packing up the whole operation and heading back to Alpha-Prime after leveling Alienn with a Defender bomb set for nuclear.

Wyatt entered ahead of Cam and they chose seats in the row of extra chairs not at the table. Hopefully, no one would notice the earthling in attendance.

Diesel gave a short introduction and explained the reason for the meeting. He then silenced the uproar, telling his brothers and the assembled elders they needed solutions not pandemonium. Once everyone settled down, one member asked, "Is there any trace of where Indigo Smith has gone? Anywhere we can start the search?"

"None. At least not yet," Diesel amended to keep himself from sinking into dire predictions.

"Does Alpha-Prime know yet?" This from his youngest brother, Jack.

"Nope. But the gulag ship is scheduled to leave tomorrow at noon. Alpha-Prime will be expecting to receive the usual message notifying them about the exact departure."

Jack said, "Around twenty hours to search an entire planet? That's typical. We should probably get started, yeah?"

"If only we knew where to start," Wheeler said, sizing up the problem perfectly in a calm, rational tone. Wheeler often had a different perspective when it came to emergency issues. Diesel appreciated his peaceful approach to most things, especially in this instance.

Abruptly, one of the elders pointed a bony finger at Wyatt. "What is an earthling doing here in this meeting?"

"He's been brought in to help us capture Indigo Smith, Mr. Gris."

"Why on earth would you do that? Bring an *earthling* into our secret fold." The elder's tone was condescending, as if earthlings were inferior by every measure and couldn't possibly help with anything.

Diesel explained, "He's an expert shot, Mr. Gris. Vastly better than anyone working at our truck stop operation."

The elderly Alpha harrumphed, as if the suggestion any earthling might have helpful attributes was an iffy proposition. "Well, don't forget, you'll have to zap his memories later."

"We know, but he's been instrumental in helping us capture nearly all of the other criminals who escaped the gulag ship."

Wyatt looked ill at ease at the mention of his memories being zapped, but didn't say anything, for which Diesel was grateful.

"Setting aside the Indigo Smith problem for the moment," Wheeler said, "I have a thought about how we can get Daphne Charlene to tell us how she found out about our alien operation here at the Big Bang Truck Stop."

"Fantastic," Diesel said. "Explain."

Wheeler grinned and gave a quick rundown of his idea. The plan included Wyatt, who looked delighted to help out despite the sullen looks thrown his way from some of the elders.

Diesel didn't know if Wheeler's idea would work, but he did an internal happy dance at the prospect of having something to do.

"Wyatt? What do you think?"

"I'm in. I want to help in any way I can."

Diesel stood up. "Nova, go check in with Gage at his lab. Help him get the faux hospital room set up and ready to clear more of Daphne Charlene's memories to before she learned about us." He looked around the room.

Nova nodded. "We also might want to call Valene in to help. She'd lend credence to our plan. I can go get her and bring her back." There were several murmurs of agreement from around the table.

Diesel held up a stalling hand. "Wait. Help Gage set up first, and you can go get Valene if needed later on."

She nodded and left the room.

Diesel adjourned the meeting and they went to set in motion Wheeler's idea to discover how Daphne Charlene learned about them. He didn't believe Wyatt had willingly given up the information.

Wyatt loved Valene, of that Diesel had no doubt, which was good since it looked like they'd recently taken their relationship to a whole new level.

At least this might be one crisis averted with only one remaining to solve. Even so, Diesel was grateful to be moving forward with any plan.

His phone buzzed. He looked at the screen. Aunt Dixie. He tipped his head back, inhaled a deep breath and answered.

"Aunt Dixie, I'm kind of busy right now."

"You're always busy, Diesel, but I wanted to let you know I'm headed out on a road trip."

Now what? "Road trip?" he asked, trying not to sound as irritated as he felt. "To where?"

She was silent for a few moments, likely deciding whether to tell him her detailed plans. "North," she said evasively.

"Why?"

"I found evidence in my attic regarding the Lost Colony Legend. I'm headed out to follow a clue."

"Oh?" Diesel started to insist she not go haring off on some adventure, but reconsidered. If his aunt Dixie was out of town, she couldn't get into trouble that he'd have to deal with.

She'd be someone else's problem for the duration and he'd be better able to concentrate on his current problems.

"That's right, I'm on the hunt to discover new information about that long-ago disastrous flight to Earth."

"Well, thanks for letting me know. Be safe and check in now and again."

"Maybe I will. Maybe I won't. I might be off grid, Diesel. I might not be able to check in regularly."

"I see. Is Miss Penny with you?"

"Yep."

Diesel sighed in relief. "Good. I'm glad you aren't going alone. Have fun."

"This is a serious mission, Diesel, not some fluffy fun trip like on the luxury liner."

"Okay, then safe travels, may the forces of good be with you and don't forget where you live."

"As if," she said and hung up.

Diesel decided Aunt Dixie being out of town during this fiasco with the prisoner escape was a blessing. She was well and truly a constant and/or looming disaster dancing with glee. With her out of town, half his daily stress went with her.

He just hoped he didn't get any calls from fellow law enforcement entities regarding her self-imposed quest along her trail north.

Wyatt readied himself to meet Daphne Charlene, Wheeler Grey's plan fresh in his head. He hated the idea of talking to or possibly touching that woman in a friendly way, but shook off his distaste.

He entered the faux hospital room, walked across the short space to the bed where she rested and leaned over her. To his right was a large mirror where Cam, Diesel and others watched through two-way glass.

"Daphne Charlene," he whispered.

Her eyes opened and she stared up at him. A smile shaped her lips. "Wyatt." She didn't even look around the room, instead gazing deeply into his eyes. "What are you doing here?"

"I came to see my best girl."

"Liar. What about Valene Grey?"

"Didn't work out. But if you aren't interested in me anymore, I won't bother you further." Wyatt took half a step back, but Daphne Charlene had faster reflexes than he imagined. She grabbed hold of one forearm, pulling on him until he moved closer.

"Of course I'm interested. I've been in love with you for months, waiting for you to lose interest in Valvoline Ethyl Grey." It occurred to Wyatt that he'd been rather slow to notice women stalking him. First Valene, now Daphne Charlene. He really should start paying better attention to his surroundings when out and about.

"Great. First, though, I need to clear something up."

Daphne Charlene frowned. "What?"

"You told Valene that you and I were together in my kitchen late last night."

She grinned. "Oh, that."

"I don't seem to remember it. I wish I could, though. What's the story?"

"Well, because I love you so much, but you haven't noticed me, I've followed you everywhere, especially in the last month or so. Last night I happened to be hiding in the woods behind your house, waiting for you to get home."

Wyatt nodded. "So that's why the dogs next door kept barking."

"Those stupid mongrels were so loud I could hardly hear myself think. But I saw you in your pajama pants when you came outside. I even saw your appendix scar when I blew up all the pictures I'd taken."

A shiver went down his spine. "Pictures?"

"Oh, yes. I have lots of pictures of you, Wyatt. Only of you. No one else is worthy." Wyatt felt the blood drain out of his face, but forced a smile and hoped she didn't notice his pallor.

"Well, isn't that nice?" No need to rile the crazy stalker.

Daphne Charlene squeezed his arm. Her adoring look made him a bit queasy, so he pressed forward. "She also said you told her a story."

Daphne Charlene frowned. "A story?"

"About space aliens at the Big Bang Truck Stop."

"Oh, that!"

"I don't remember telling you anything like that

last night nor do I remember meeting you in my kitchen."

"Oh, you didn't. And we didn't meet in your kitchen. I only told Valene that to make her jealous. It worked, too."

"Who told you that story about aliens and the Big Bang Truck Stop?"

"Rowan told me."

"Rowan? Who's that?"

"He's my new, very good friend." Daphne Charlene suddenly sat bolt upright, grabbing Wyatt by both arms, her fingers digging into his flesh through his shirt. "But I don't love him like I love you, Wyatt."

Wyatt cupped her elbows in his palms and gently eased her back to the raised bed. "Of course not. I know that." He patted her arm awkwardly, as she still had a grip on him. She seemed to settle down after a few seconds and leaned back on the bed.

Wyatt stayed where he was alongside her. "Where did you meet Rowan?"

"He came to my place."

"Your home?"

"No, silly. My Critter's Café place." *Right, your roadkill restaurant on the hill.*

"He loved my award-winning chili recipe."

"Who wouldn't?"

"He ate three bowls."

"He must have been hungry," Wyatt said. "Why

did Rowan say there were space aliens at the truck stop?"

"He was just making fun. He was convinced that if I told that to the owner, Diesel Grey, that it would be a great joke." She laughed uproariously.

"Funny," Wyatt agreed and laughed as best he could with her. "How does Rowan know Diesel?"

Her face screwed up into an unpleasant frown. "I'm not sure, but Diesel would have to know him to get the joke, wouldn't he?" She paused as if thinking hard about that. "Well, they must be old friends or something." She looked a bit unsure, then shook it off and gazed deeply into Wyatt's eyes. "I want you to know that once I help Rowan get a new ID, because his was lost in an unfortunate house fire back home, that he'll be on his way to a new town up north and you won't have to worry about my affections for him. I know you must be a teeny bit jealous. Admit it."

"Maybe just a little." Wyatt asked, managing a half smile, "Rowan is going north, huh? Does he have a job up there, wherever he's going?"

Daphne Charlene nodded. "Yep. He's going to be a guard. That's what he does right now. You know, he guards stuff. When he moves up north, he'll be a guard doing more guarding of stuff." She laughed again as the door opened behind him.

Gage and Nova entered. Daphne Charlene grinned at them. "Who are you?"

"I'm your nurse," Nova said.

"But I thought you were Diesel's secretary."

"I prefer the term executive assistant, but I only do that in my spare time. Most of the time I'm a nurse."

"Gotcha." To Gage, she said, "Does that mean you're my doctor?"

"Sort of. Actually, I'm more of a scientist, but one day I might be a doctor."

"But the really important question is…do you play a doctor on TV?" Daphne Charlene asked and fell back against the pillow, laughing wildly at her own joke.

"The Defender works differently on some humans," Gage told Wyatt, as if to explain Daphne Charlene's odd behavior. "Cam sent a message to Axel to look into any guards with the name Rowan or similar on the gulag ship's manifest, current and prior."

Daphne Charlene laughed again. "Gulag? What a funny word! It's so hilarious." She giggled harder.

"This must be the laughing gas version of Daphne Charlene," Nova mumbled. "I'm still not a fan."

"Behave, Nova." Gage started to fiddle with some of the controls on the machine he was about to attach Daphne Charlene to.

"Yeah, behave, Nova," Daphne Charlene parroted. She laughed again.

Wyatt backed away from the bed as Gage and

Nova moved to stand on either side of the giddy woman. They each grabbed an arm. Daphne Charlene didn't put up any protest. Her gaze was locked on Wyatt. He stared back to ensure she didn't realize what they were doing.

"Better leave the room, Wyatt," Gage said, waving the Defender at his side. "Don't want to accidentally have any Defender beams bouncing around in here hit you."

"Right." Wyatt turned and exited the faux hospital room as Daphne Charlene started wailing. He was unmoved by her screams, the ones he heard even after he was out of the room. Just outside the door, Cam and Diesel stood in front of the two-way window, quietly conversing. They looked at him, but didn't invite him over and continued chatting in low tones.

After only a few seconds, Daphne Charlene stopped shrieking. Wyatt assumed she'd been quieted by a Defender blast. That was also *his* future unless he found Valene or at least got a chance to talk to her before they erased his memories. He'd have to convince her to marry him and then move two galaxies away.

If by some miracle all that worked out, what in the world would he do on Alpha-Prime if he went there? What job could an earthling get? Would a law enforcement position of some sort be available? This and a thousand other questions swirled in his head.

Another shout rose up inside the room. It sounded like Nova. Cam and Diesel raced into the room. Wyatt walked to the window to watch, but couldn't quite figure out what was going on.

Nova was pointing to a sleeping Daphne Charlene, talking fast and making all kinds of arm gestures. His sister Sally was like that, too. If someone tied her arms down, he didn't think she'd be able to talk at all.

Whatever the hubbub was, Cam and Diesel were talking and Nova was nodding.

Nova soon exited Daphne Charlene's room, followed by Cam and Diesel. She took off her white nurse's jacket and placed it on a coatrack just outside the door.

Wyatt knew better than to ask what had just gone on, so instead he asked, "Want me to go get Valene, now? I don't mind."

Nova looked at Cam and Diesel. They both frowned, then continued talking in front of the two-way window again. Everyone looked like something dire had happened.

She shook her head. "Best not. Don't worry. I'll get Valene from her home and bring her right back. She'll be glad to know that you have been exonerated regarding the tattling about Alphas and our basement operation. I know she'll be especially happy to learn for certain that you didn't have a secret rendezvous with Daphne Charlene in your kitchen last night."

Wyatt's eyes closed. He'd forgotten she didn't know about that yet. Was she still hurt, thinking he'd cheated on her?

"She didn't truly believe it anyway," Nova said. Her sheepish grin told him she might have just read his mind.

"Still, I'd love for her to have proof positive." Was that why she'd been flirting with that guy earlier? And if she did forgive him and wasn't flirting with someone else, what did that mean?

If only that guaranteed him a life with her.

After Nova left, Diesel and Cam motioned for Wyatt to join them. Through the glass, he saw a sleeping Daphne Charlene being loaded onto a gurney.

"Thanks for the help, Wyatt." Diesel started to say something else, but his phone rang. He looked at the number, sighed deeply and excused himself to take the call in his office.

"What happens to her now?" Wyatt asked Cam, even though he probably should keep a low profile, stay quiet and hope they didn't blast his memories away when he least expected it.

"She'll be transported to her home and placed on her sofa. She'll be awake in an hour or so. We'll have someone keep an eye on her for a couple days to make sure she's okay."

Wyatt nodded. He didn't like the woman, but he didn't want anything bad to happen to her. "What will happen once Valene gets here?"

"We'll all have to sit down and have a discussion," Cam said. "Nova saw something in Daphne Charlene's mind right before her memories were erased."

"I'm afraid to ask," Wyatt said. "Did she see the guard, Rowan, or whatever his name is? Did she know who it was?"

"Possibly. But Nova saw the flash of a face in her head and thought it might be Indigo Smith. That's why she shouted. Now, she's not so certain. And if it *is* him, he's in disguise."

"Disguise?"

"Yeah. Indigo Smith has dark hair and big blue eyes. Supposedly, that's why he's able to get away with so much. Nova said the face that flashed through Daphne Charlene's mind looked like him, but had white-blond hair and a piercing green gaze."

Wyatt perked up. "I've seen that guy. Or at least a guy with that description."

Cam stilled. "Where?"

"When we first got back, Gage was watching the surveillance video of the truck stop convenience store. The blond guy was the flirty customer talking Valene up in the Maxwell the Martian aisle when we got back with the hairy alien."

"Where was I?" Cam asked.

Wyatt shrugged. "Taking care of the hairy alien, I guess. I don't know." Cam walked over to a computer terminal in Gage's lab. He searched several surveillance camera feeds until he found the footage Wyatt had seen earlier with Gage. Valene had apparently been talking with the guy for over twenty minutes before they returned. Daphne Charlene could be seen in the background pacing in front of the cash register with a foul expression on her face as she watched Valene chat with Mr. Flirty.

"When Nova gets back with Valene, we'll have to see if this is the dude she saw."

Wyatt wasn't certain he wanted to traipse around looking for the guy Valene had been flirting with, but remained silent.

"What if that face was only in Daphne Charlene's mind because that's who Valene was talking to right before she got zapped by the Defender?"

Cam pondered that for a moment. "I guess it's possible."

He searched through more surveillance feeds, but didn't seem to find what he was looking for, if his sour attitude was any indication.

Nova came running into the lab. "Valene's gone!"

"What do you mean she's gone? Where is she?"

"I don't know and I mean she's not at home, or at your parents' home or anywhere in Alienn that I could find on my way back."

"Did you call her cell?" Cam asked, reaching for his phone.

Nova held up her hand to show her cell phone

clutched in one palm. "Yes. Of course, she isn't picking up. I called so many times to leave, 'Call me back' messages that her voice mail is already full."

In Nova's other hand was a piece of paper. She held it up. "Plus, I found this note taped on Valene's front door."

"Way to bury the lead, Nova."

"Don't mess with me, I'm worried sick about her."

Wyatt was also horribly worried about Valene.

Cam took the note from Nova and read out loud, "Hey, Fearless Leader. I'm fairly certain that I have something you want. Just like you have something that I want. Let's meet tonight at midnight at the lovers' lane and make the exchange or else your little sister will remain with me permanently and the two of us will enjoy this fine new planet together, tucked away where I promise you will never find us. I.S."

"What does he want?" Wyatt asked, his fists clenching and unclenching at his sides. If he knew where to go and rescue her, Wyatt would already be running in that direction, alien purple goo splatter gun at the ready to take down Indigo Smith.

"I wish I knew."

Nova pushed out a long sigh. "I'll bet Daphne Charlene knew before we zapped her memories into oblivion."

Chapter 11

Valene blinked sedately as she rode in the passenger seat of her sports car, watching the scenery go by. She felt really good. Peaceful. Serene. And a bit whimsical, truth be told. Had she ever felt this way before? Maybe, but she couldn't remember any specifics. Her memories faded like the remnants of a powerful dream upon waking. At first, the images are so clear and rational. But as reality sets in, the truth of riding a giant tiger with a saddle on his back to work like everyone does it every day becomes a silly notion. Even so, she enjoyed the serenity and watching the trees go by outside the window.

Was she dreaming right now? She wasn't sure. Maybe.

She looked at the handsome man driving the car. Where were they going again? She tried to muster the energy to ask. After clearing her suddenly very dry throat and opening her mouth to speak, Valene couldn't recall what she'd been about to say. Hmm.

The man smiled, raised his eyebrows as if waiting for her to say something, but she was lost for words. How embarrassing. Better not to speak until she knew what she wanted to say, right?

Valene smiled at him, shook her head and put her focus back out her side window and the rustic scenery along the road, settling comfortably into her seat. She closed her eyes and tried to remember her question, but the details evaded her until she decided a nap was a good idea. She let go and started to fall into a light slumber.

Maybe she'd try and remember whatever it was later. Or maybe not. Either way, sleep was so much more important.

Earlier, after watching only a few seconds of the surveillance video of Valene with the handsome stranger, Wyatt had wanted to sneak out the secret alien side door, run around to the convenience store's front entrance and get between Valene and Mr. Suave and Flirty. But Gage wouldn't let him. A dangerous alien criminal had been right there, and he'd gotten away without anyone there to stop him. And now Valene was missing.

Diesel's shoulders slumped after he read Indigo Smith's note. Then he pulled himself together and ordered everyone to the conference room. Diesel, Gage, Nova, Wyatt, and Cam all trooped inside.

Wheeler, Jack and Axel arrived moments later, apparently summoned when Wyatt wasn't paying attention. Must be a secure area so that no humans—not invited in like he was—could overhear any alien plots.

As soon as they were seated around the table, everyone started talking at once.

Jack said, "We need to get out there and start looking until she's found, yeah?"

"Yeah!" Wheeler nodded and poked Axel, who nodded and added his own, "Yeah!" to the cacophony in the room.

Diesel put two fingers to his lips and whistled loud enough to settle them down. "One at a time. Nova, what did you see?"

Gage held up the screenshot of the guy who'd been chatting with Valene in the convenience store with the light hair. Nova pointed at it. "That's the guy I saw in Daphne Charlene's head right before we zapped her memories away."

"Is that Indigo Smith?" Axel asked.

Diesel nodded. "His hair and eye color have been drastically changed, but yes, it's him. I don't understand why Valene wouldn't recognize him."

"Maybe he's charming," Nova offered. "I mean, don't get me wrong. I wouldn't fall for a known criminal, but he's not hard to look at."

"Charming enough to keep anyone from recognizing his true identity?" Cam asked.

Gage said, "I didn't recognize him earlier when I saw the footage."

"Me, either."

There was a knock at the door. Diesel shouted, "Enter!"

Bubba Thorne and the pale bounty hunter, Luther Boudreaux, came in and seated themselves at the table.

Diesel nodded at the two. "I asked Bubba and Luther to join us to help hunt down our final prisoner." He passed Luther, who sat closest to him, the note left on Valene's door. "It goes without saying that my sister's abduction changes things. I want to ensure she isn't caught in any crossfire. We don't exactly know what Indigo Smith is prepared to do, but I'm certain that he will be very resistant to our plan to capture, shackle and ensure he's headed for that gulag as soon as possible."

Bubba asked, "What happened to your sister?"

"Our final prisoner has abducted her and left a note that he wants to meet tonight."

Luther grimaced as he read the note and handed it to Bubba. Diesel played the video clip from the convenience store on the smart board.

"Does your sister know this man?" Luther asked. "Her body language seems to indicate she's familiar with him."

"Not to my knowledge," Diesel said at the same time Wyatt said, "Of course she doesn't know him."

"You're the boyfriend," Luther said matter-of-factly.

"Fiancé," Wyatt corrected.

"Right. Sorry. And you're certain she's never met him before?"

"Fairly certain. Yes."

"Interesting."

"What is?"

Luther looked around the table. Everyone was staring at him. Wyatt tried not to glare, but it wasn't easy.

"I'm a bounty hunter by trade and I've spent quite a bit of time studying the body language of Alphas, other humanoids and a whole range of creatures while waiting to capture my prey to bring them to justice. Your sister's body language is classic for not only knowing this man, but trusting him."

"How can that be?" Wyatt asked, feeling rather surly that Valene was in fact looking at the handsome criminal much like she looked at *him*. "Even if Indigo Smith met with her as he popped out of his cryo-tube thing, she wouldn't trust him as far as she could throw him in only a day and a half."

No one said anything.

Wyatt searched his mind for any possible explanation. "Wait. What if she's been shackled?"

"What?" Diesel and Cam said at the same time.

"What if Indigo Smith found a way to shackle her? What if she's only going along with him because she has to? Because she's been made to. Because her will is not her own. Sort of like Daphne Charlene seemed to be when she was here."

Every face at the table registered horror as they considered the implications of that scenario.

"Space potatoes." Cam said the words like a curse and stood up. Wyatt didn't know what space potatoes were, but assumed the phrase was like alien swearing. The look in Cam's eyes bordered on panic.

Axel shook his head. "Shackle stickers aren't available to just anyone." But Valene's brother didn't sound very confident of that.

Bubba and Luther looked at each other as if they'd solved a mystery. Bubba said, "But they are now standard issue on any and all gulag transports, are they not? If there is a dirty Royal Magistrate Guardsman involved, and we don't know that for certain yet, perhaps it would be prudent to check the prison ship's inventory."

"Regardless of why Valene is with him and even if her being shackled makes a lot of sense, we still don't know what he wants in trade, do we?" Wheeler asked.

Wyatt stood. "Wait. Could it be the new ID Daphne Charlene was going to get her new friend Rowan because his house burned down?"

Diesel snapped his fingers. "That is a distinct possibility. What else could it be? But I'm not sure how he plans to get away even with a fake ID.

We'd still all know and be able to look for him, right?"

Cam said, "The truth is we don't know exactly what Indigo Smith is capable of. He's managed to escape every single time he's been captured, including this time. He's rumored to be a genius across several fields of study. I doubted that, but not anymore."

"What's our best plan of action?" Bubba asked.

"We'll have to get the ID from Daphne Charlene, right?" Wyatt asked the obvious question and everyone nodded. "We have to take the fake ID to the bauxite pit and trade it for Valene."

"We should also thoroughly search Daphne Charlene's place, if that's where Mr. Smith has been hiding all this time right under our noses," Cam added. "Maybe he left behind a clue as to his next earthly destination."

Diesel rolled his eyes. "Don't get your hopes up, but yeah, let's all of us head over there and take a look."

"Will she be awake from her memory wipe?" Wyatt asked. He needed to bear up if he had to pretend to like her again. "Also, how much of her memory was zapped?"

"Only to the day before the gulag ship arrived to erase her memories of Rowan a.k.a. Indigo," Gage answered.

"Did anyone ever find a guard named Rowan registered on the ship?" Cam asked.

Diesel shook his head. "Not yet. I checked. No Rowan or any name even close to it on the gulag manifest for either guards or prisoners. Probably a fake name he came up with."

"Note to self, Rowan is another alias of Indigo Smith," Bubba said.

"Great. What are we doing?" Wyatt tried not to sound so impatient, but he was vibrating with the urgency to go find Valene, rescue her and put his fist into Mr. Flirty's face. "Because if nobody has a good plan beyond wrestling the ID from Daphne Charlene and meeting this infamous prisoner later on *his* schedule, I'm going to go stake out the bauxite pit's lovers' lane until he shows up with Valene and take him out before the trade even takes place."

"How?"

"I'm going to take my shiny new alien purple goo splatter gun and put a pellet in the center of his white toothy grin."

"Admirable," Diesel said. "But only if he doesn't use our sister as a shield."

"Of course not." Wyatt would never aim a gun near Valene.

"You should go to Daphne Charlene's and get the ID, if it's there. Maybe you'll find more information as well," Nova said. "Wyatt here will be able to get any and all information from her. She adores him."

Wyatt sighed deeply. "Lucky me."

Diesel's phone buzzed again. He ignored it. "Okay, here's what we're going to do. Gage, Wheeler, Jack and Nova go see if you can figure out how Mr. Smith escaped the gulag ship and if any of the guards or anyone else helped him. Also check the shackle sticker inventory there. Tear the ship down to the metal plating if you have to.

"Bubba, you and Luther join Cam, Wyatt, Axel and me. We'll go search Daphne Charlene's place for the fake ID and any other clues as to what Mr. Smith is planning." He checked his phone for the time. "We'll all meet back here in three hours to figure out what we're going to do at the meeting to trade for Valene."

Wyatt knew what he was going to do, as long as they allowed him access to that goo splatter gun. Pow! A purple pellet planted right between that criminal's big stupid front teeth.

Chapter 12

Valene stirred awake slowly after what seemed like a troubled sleep. Her head ached and she couldn't remember where she was or what time it was or even what day it was.

Am I sick?

"Valene," a hauntingly familiar voice said.

Her eyes opened and she saw him. He smiled at her. Then she remembered...a little.

Wyatt's spine stiffened as he knocked on Daphne Charlene's door. *Don't forget to be nice. Don't forget to be nice.*

She answered after keeping him waiting for excruciatingly long seconds. She looked like she'd just woken from a long, unexpected nap. The moment she saw him, she perked up. "Wyatt! What are you doing here?" She opened the door wider and motioned him inside. He pulled the screen open, and stepped across her threshold, purposely leaving the front door open.

"I was in the neighborhood and wondered if you were free for lunch."

"Really?"

"Yes."

"What about Valene?"

"Didn't work out," he lied again.

Wyatt didn't know what was going to happen between him and Valene ultimately. He did know it was very difficult to pretend any interest in Daphne Charlene when he was worried sick about Valene.

Was she hurt? Was she afraid? Did she miss him? His blood pressure rose at the mere thought of anything negative with regard to his love, so he tried to settle his mind as another thought occurred. Valene didn't even know he'd been proven innocent of tattling about aliens living in plain sight or the lie about what happened in his kitchen last night. Yet.

Wyatt looked around the living room, wondering where Daphne Charlene would keep a fake ID for a friend and also how to ask her to reveal it.

Across the room, he spotted a small open rolltop desk with rows of cubbies and little doors. Centered on the open surface was a brown paper-wrapped package. "Is that a package you received or one you're sending," he asked, pointing to the parcel. Was it the infamous ID they were supposed to trade tonight?

She turned to see where he pointed and made a face, like the package puzzled her. "I'm not sure." She walked to the desk as Wyatt followed, motioning with a deft hand behind his back for the others to enter quietly.

Daphne Charlene looked down at the package and frowned. "I've never seen this before."

In the center was the name Rowan. "The return address is yours," Wyatt said, running his finger over it. "Who is Rowan?"

"I don't know. Maybe it was delivered to me by accident."

Before he could stop her, she picked it up and shook it like a Christmas present and she was a kid trying to discover the treasure inside.

Wyatt didn't think that was a very good idea and pulled the box from her, placing it gently back on the desk. "Don't do that to a strange package." She shrugged and moved closer to him.

He pulled his trusty pocketknife out and slit the loosely applied paper off one end to slide a shoebox out.

"Wait. That's my shoebox."

Wyatt carefully lifted the lid to peek inside. There were no shoes in there.

He felt rather than heard the others approach.

"What's inside the box?" Diesel asked.

Daphne Charlene shrieked in surprise as she

saw five more men had entered her living room. "What are you all doing here?"

Wyatt tilted the open shoebox toward Diesel so he could see the megaphone inside, or rather the alien Defender. Indigo Smith obviously planned to shoot any humans along his getaway path in order to escape. He sure was resourceful to have gotten not only shackle stickers but also a Defender. Perhaps there really was some guard involved.

Daphne Charlene reached inside the shoebox before Wyatt could stop her and grabbed the device. If she pulled the trigger, they'd both be on the ground for an undetermined length of time.

"It's just a mini megaphone," she said, and pulled the trigger before Wyatt could stop her.

Wyatt's eyes slammed shut and he braced himself to fall to the ground like last time in Cam's office. He heard the thud as something heavy hit the ground, but after a count of three, was surprised to find he remained on his feet.

"That's odd," Daphne Charlene said. "Why did they all fall to the ground in a faint?"

His eyes popped open to see Diesel, Cam, Axel and Bubba on the ground like human dominoes, or rather alien. Luther was still on his feet, but had drawn his Defender.

"How are you not on the ground?" Wyatt asked.

"I'm from a different..." His gaze went to Daphne Charlene. "Uhm...country than they are."

"Did I kill them?" Daphne Charlene's voice was

shrill. "I didn't mean to kill them," she said, waving the altered Defender around.

Luther raised his weapon and pointed it at Daphne Charlene.

"Wait." Wyatt put a hand up to stop Luther. "I've got this."

Wyatt calmed Daphne Charlene and convinced her it would be a good idea to lie down and rest in her bedroom. Once he accompanied her there, he insisted she hadn't killed anyone as he carefully pried the Defender from her fingers.

By the time he returned to the living room, Luther had dropped to one knee to check that Diesel, Axel, Cam and Bubba were still breathing. He gave Wyatt a thumbs-up.

Wyatt put the obviously altered Defender back in the shoebox and put the lid on it securely. Turning back to the desk, he studied all the little square cubbies until he found the ID.

Yanking a laminated card from the lowest left-hand cubby, Wyatt studied it. It was an Arkansas driver's license with an Indigo Smith picture, sporting his natural dark hair and blue eyes.

He held the card up and read, "Dane Gareth Asher."

Luther said, "Well, at least we have what Indigo wants to trade for Valene."

Wyatt was about to ask what they should do about the four Alphas crumpled on Daphne Charlene's living room carpet when Bubba coughed and sat up. "What in the space potato farm just happened to me?"

Wyatt lifted the shoebox. "Looks like our celebrity prisoner altered the technology in a stolen Defender and made it work on Alphas."

"That's unexpected. And terrible." Bubba rubbed his temples with both hands. "The abominable headache side effect isn't very sporting, either."

Diesel and Cam soon roused with the same aching heads and horrified attitude over what Indigo Smith had apparently accomplished.

Axel was last to wake up. He groaned. "Who hit me in the head with the freight train?" Bubba helped him to his feet, but the big Guardsman and Valene's brothers all looked like the before picture on a pain relief commercial.

Wyatt held up the ID. "This is the ID Daphne Charlene somehow found for him." He held up the shoebox. "And this is the altered Defender."

"Where's Daphne Charlene?" Diesel asked.

"She was freaking out because she thought she killed you all so I put her in her bedroom to rest. She fell asleep the moment she was horizontal."

"A symptom of the other mind wipe we did, probably." Cam sighed. "We'll have to blast her with the Defender again to cover the time we were here."

"It won't hurt her, will it?" Wyatt asked. He didn't see the need to punish her unduly.

"No. Unlike the reverse-engineered Defender

used on us, it doesn't cause splitting headaches," Cam assured him. "It will make her sleepy, though."

Wyatt nodded. "Well, she's already asleep, so it won't change anything."

Bubba had the shoebox with the Defender opened up and was looking at it. "He really is a diabolical genius, isn't he?"

"I'm afraid to ask, but how long were we out?" Cam asked, adjusting the setting on his Defender.

"Only a couple of minutes."

"How long have we been here in total?" he asked as he fiddled with the dial on his Defender.

"Eleven minutes," Bubba said, checking his digital wristwatch.

Cam finished making the adjustments on his Defender, and headed for Daphne Charlene's bedroom door.

"Now what?" Wyatt asked when they were all back in Diesel's vehicle, headed to the Big Bang Truck Stop.

"We have just over five hours before the meeting. We should spend our time discussing our plans for later tonight."

"Plans?" Cam asked.

"Given the wily nature of our escaped celebrity prisoner and his recently discovered abilities, we need more than one plan in place. We not only need a primary plan, we need several backup plans, too."

Nova greeted them at the basement door as they all walked inside.

"Don't tell me you have more bad news," Diesel said.

She rolled her eyes. "I'm sorry, bad news is the only thing we're selling these days."

"What is it?"

"The head of the United Galactic Gulag has left three messages already. It seems there are some nervous leaders on Alpha-Prime who have tasked him with providing an update ensuring that the gulag ship docked here—with the most infamous criminal ever caught hibernating on board—will leave on time tomorrow morning without incident. Additionally, he'd love to have some sort of proof, like a picture or, better yet, a short video of Indigo Smith sound asleep in his cryo-pod."

Chapter 13

Valene opened her eyes and sat up in a strange bed. She searched the elegantly appointed room for a clue as to where she was and why she was here. Everything in the room was of high quality and looked expensive. But nothing was familiar. Perhaps her brain had not caught up to the party just yet. Maybe she needed a coffee or another glass of sweet tea.

She remembered Aunt Dixie cutting her off after ordering the third large Mason jar full of her favorite beverage at the Cosmos Café, insisting she'd be up all night going to the bathroom. Valene chuckled to herself for two seconds until the urge to pee made her stand up and search for a bathroom. She saw three doors on three different walls of the generously sized room. The first choice and closest was the bathroom she gratefully sought.

Back in the bedroom a few minutes later, she checked the second door and found an empty walk-in closet the size of a small bedroom. *Nice.*

The third door on the other side of the room turned out to be locked.

She rattled the handle and pounded on the surface of the door, shouting for someone to let her out.

No such luck.

She wandered around the luxurious room, noting sunlight spilling through the three narrow windows high up on one wall. They looked like the kind of windows sometimes put in basements, but this room didn't feel like it was in a basement. It was lovely.

Fatigue sent her back to sit on the foot of the bed where she'd started. Maybe she'd take a nap while she waited to figure out what to do next. It seemed like she should do something, but the need for more sleep blocked almost everything else out.

Valene gave in to the seeming need for more rest, scooting back to put her head on the pillow. Her eyes closed, but the nagging wish to remember where she was kept her from falling into slumber.

Why was she here? Where had she been before the Cosmos Café? At the truck stop? Yes. She'd been upstairs about to talk to Daphne Charlene. *Oh! That woman.*

But Diesel showed up unexpectedly and sent her to Cam's office. Wyatt had been there, but Cam entered soon after and shot him with a Defender. He'd crumpled at her feet.

Her troubling memories seeped in one by one, each seemingly more disturbing than the last. The insinuation that Wyatt and Daphne Charlene had been intimate in Wyatt's kitchen while Valene was asleep in his bedroom thumped the loudest in her mind. The further implication that Wyatt had tattled to the odious woman about aliens living in plain sight at the truck stop made Valene's thoughts come to a full stop. He wouldn't do that.

Valene knew Wyatt. She'd followed him for nearly two years before making accidental contact. Not every day, though. She wasn't a psycho, but she'd kept tabs on him and his life. He was a good guy liked by most everyone. He put a monthly rundown of what was going on in Skeeter Bite on the official Skeeter Bite Sheriff's Office website and also covered what was to come in the next month. Each and every month she looked forward to the rundowns. She found his monthly "Activities in Skeeter Bite" entries charming. She also found Wyatt very charming.

For all intents and purposes, Wyatt Campbell was a stand-up sheriff, an honorable man, a crack shot with a rifle and he was the sweetest boyfriend she'd ever had. True, he was the *only* boyfriend she'd ever had, but why look elsewhere once you've found perfection?

Valene must have drifted off and slept for quite a while because when she woke up, it was dark and shadowy in the room. The little sunlight from the windows had faded dramatically to a few orange lines along one wall.

A loud hollow bang, like the sound of a dead bolt being thrown, echoed through the room, shaking Valene awake. She sat up and threw her legs over the edge of the bed. She felt light-headed, sure that if she stood up, she'd end up on the floor. She straightened her back and remained seated.

The blond man from the car came into the room. He closed the door behind him, grabbed the chair from a desk across the room, placed it in front of her and seated himself next to the bed.

"Good evening, sleepyhead," he said with a soothing smile.

"Where are we?" Valene asked, feeling a rise of panic. She shouldn't be here. She shouldn't be with any man but Wyatt, especially in a bedroom.

This was wrong. This was *all* wrong. Her lips pressed flat as she considered how she could get past him and out the now unbolted bedroom door.

The man, obviously seeing her trepidation, leaned forward and pegged her with his intense stare as if beseeching her to remain calm. His gaze was intensely focused on her eyes, but he didn't speak. He simply smiled.

Valene's alarm melted like ice cubes plunged into boiling water. No worries here.

Her posture relaxed and the fuzzy fog came back, filling her with a lack of urgency. Why had she been so worked up? She couldn't remember. It must not matter.

Valene smiled. "What are we going to do now? Take another car ride?"

"Yes. And we'll have to leave very soon," he said quietly.

Valene didn't even know where she was right now and, truthfully, she didn't care. One place was as good as another. "Where are we going for our car ride?"

"To the lovers' lane by the bauxite mine. We'll meet some friends there."

Valene nodded. She knew where that was. She'd been there with Wyatt once a while back when her brother Axel's wedding was being planned.

The abrupt and distinct memory of passionately kissing Wyatt in his patrol car at that very location slid clearly past whatever fog filled her brain. The fog began to dissipate slowly and other memories began to appear.

After only a few seconds, she remembered *exactly* who this man was.

Indigo Smith. *Space potatoes. Why am I in this strange bedroom with him?*

Her brothers had thought the escaped convict might already be in another country by now.

Valene wanted to run like a maddened sand-claw beast was seconds from clutching her in its steely sharp-nailed grasp, but she forced herself to be calm. She mentally took a deep breath, put a serene smile in place and nodded. "Good. I'd like to meet some friends."

The blond man stopped staring at her and the last of the mental fog dissipated like sunlight burning directly through the morning mist, giving her a clear mind once more.

Indigo Smith had some sort of mental power and the unique ability to wield it over Alphas. Valene had never heard of any alien able to do that. Miss Penny could change her form, but didn't have any mental abilities that Valene knew of.

His unique skill at putting suggestible fog into people's minds to make them trust him had likely been very handy for a criminal. It also must be why he'd been able to escape from every place he'd ever been locked up. Indigo looked away and reached into his pocket, retrieving a cell phone.

Valene searched the room for a fixed focal point to keep her wits about her. She found and stared at the bathroom doorknob, keeping her features serene. It was difficult, but she didn't want the fog machine to start up again. Thinking about Wyatt kept her mind clear. The recent memories of Daphne Charlene and her lies reared up to make Valene mad at herself. Of course Wyatt would never tell anyone about aliens living in plain sight. Of course he would never slink off and spend time with Daphne Charlene in his kitchen while Valene slept in his bed. How could she have ever been so foolish?

Because it was easier to let him go with fake and foolish anger, even though deep down inside she didn't believe it. That's what she'd been pondering as she sucked down the better part of three large sweet tea drinks before Indigo Smith showed up to put a mental fog spell into her mind.

"First, though, we need to make a phone call," he told her.

"Okay."

Indigo Smith dialed the number and pushed the button for the speakerphone feature as Valene watched him, wondering why she'd ever fallen for this man. She forced herself not to think about it, and instead considered bashing this wily criminal over the head with the nearby lamp and running for her life.

She didn't know where she was. It was better to go along until she had some sort of plan.

The other party picked up and Valene heard a sleepy Daphne Charlene answer, "Hello?"

"Hello," Indigo said in a slightly different voice than he'd used with Valene. "It's Rowan. It's time to meet like we talked about. I'd like to pick up that special item we discussed as well as the package I left on your desk. Is my ID ready?"

"Rowan who?" Valene's archnemesis asked. Subtly, Valene tried to search her surroundings. If she saw a way to get away safely, she'd take it.

"I don't know anybody named Rowan," Daphne Charlene said.

Indigo frowned. His voice changed to a melodic tone. Valene closed her eyes and listened to the soothing cadence of his voice. It was mesmerizing.

"Daphne, it's me, Rowan. Don't you remember who I am? We spent some lovely time together. You helped me change my looks. I pretended to be someone you cared about and you did me a favor. Do you remember?"

Valene's mind filled with mist as he spoke, but this time she was aware of what was happening. This time she didn't lose her recent realization. The fog didn't take any of her precious memories of Wyatt.

There was a silence for several seconds before Daphne Charlene said, "Nope." There was a loud click as she disconnected the call.

Indigo said a vile Alpha curse and shoved his cell phone back into his pocket. He stood and paced. Valene sat quietly staring at the bathroom doorknob.

Keep it together. Don't let him know you aren't under his spell. Valene forced herself to relax and keep a smile in place. "Is it time to go meet those friends?"

He stopped pacing. "Yes. But we need to make a stop first."

Valene stood up, her stupid goofy smile held firm. *Keep it together. I can do this.*

Indigo stared then gave her a new sort of smile.

The same kind of smile that Wyatt had given her many times before. A smile of love. *Oh no.*

Indigo Smith stepped closer, leaning in as if he planned to kiss her. *Not happening, dude.*

The moment his lips brushed her cheek, she flinched. *Space potatoes.*

Indigo frowned and drew away. In his mesmerizing gaze, she saw that he knew.

Cue the fog machine.

Chapter 14

Wyatt thought hard about recent events all the way to the Big Bang Truck Stop basement. Something didn't add up. Well, lots of things didn't add up, starting with aliens living in plain sight in Arkansas for the past umpteen years without him noticing, but something else had been nagging at him.

Nova's bombshell announcement regarding wanting proof of Indigo Smith still being in his cryo-pod had spooked the others.

Diesel barked orders like a field marshal, sending Cam to Gage's lab for an update. He then sent Axel, Bubba and Luther off to the gulag ship for additional information and an expressed wish they return soon with answers. No one even knew what answers to look for, but everyone did what their Fearless Leader ordered them to do.

"Wyatt," Diesel said, obviously about to send him on a task.

"Wait. Before you send me off, hear me out. Something has been bothering me."

"Only one thing?" Diesel said sarcastically.

Wyatt couldn't help the grin. "Yes. I'm wondering about the timeline."

"Timeline?"

"You sent Valene home. If she got there or not, there was a note pasted there, right?"

"Right."

"Indigo Smith left the note that he wanted something we had to make a trade for Valene."

"Yes. So?"

"So we only just now got the ID and altered Defender. He already had Valene by then. The question is, what didn't he have that we are supposed to bring for the trade?"

"That's a good question." Diesel's eyes narrowed. "You're right. I've been so freaked out about Smith being loose, and kidnapping my sister that I'm losing my ability to think clearly."

"Maybe I just have a unique perspective."

"Maybe you do."

"What could he want, keeping in mind he likely planned to stop off at Daphne Charlene's to pick those things up before meeting us on the lovers' lane?"

"I wish I knew."

Diesel's phone buzzed. "Bubba? What's up?" He pushed the speaker button so Wyatt could hear, too.

"Gage found something interesting in the computer files from the gulag ship and sent us a message to check it out."

"Okay."

"We found something truly, well, unexpected on the prisoner ship. I think you need to get over here to see it with your own eyes. In fact, we found more than one thing."

"What did you find?"

"I don't think you'll believe what I'm about to tell you unless you see if for yourself."

"Tell me anyway."

"You know the five prisoners that didn't make it out of their pods during the solar flare incident."

"Sure. Those were five we didn't have to go out and find wandering on Earth. I was grateful."

"Well, it turns out that they are not prisoners."

"I don't understand."

"Each of the five pods had a special computer simulation card embedded in the controls so it looked like a prisoner was in there. Not anymore. Gage was able to disrupt the sim card to reveal what is really in the cryo-pods."

"What in the space potato farm is in there if not prisoners?"

"Ingots."

Diesel frowned like he didn't understand the word. "Say that again." The only ingots Wyatt knew about were gold ingots.

"Alpha-Prime grade A gold ingots, ten pounds each, stamped with the symbol from the main branch of the largest depository in Alpha-Prime's premium sphere. Each of the five cryo-pods is filled to the top with carefully stacked ingots."

"Gold ingots?" Wyatt asked. "You all have gold on your planet, too? Is it a treasure like here on Earth?"

"Yes, sort of a treasure. But it's used very differently on Alpha-Prime."

"What do you use gold for?"

"Alternate fuel source."

Valene was caught. Indigo overpowered her, pushed her to the bed, smashed her face into the soft surface and had her in Alpha handcuffs bound behind her back before she even realized he'd moved.

So frustrating.

"I don't understand why you are immune to my charms, Valene. Even the weak humans here on this lovely planet bend to my will as easily as the Alphas back home."

She didn't know, either, but wondered how she could ever have fallen for him in the first place. Wyatt was her love. Her only love.

Indigo Smith, devious and infamous Alpha criminal, didn't hold a candle to the honorable, sweet human sheriff Wyatt Campbell, who had captured her heart long ago. How was she ever swayed by this dastardly gulag-bound alien?

"Maybe you aren't as charming as you think

you are," she said, adopting a new attitude. He pulled her off the bed, but she struggled, doing her best to gain her freedom.

"Stop it!" Indigo yanked her up, grabbed both arms and squeezed. "Don't fight me or you'll be riding in the trunk of the car."

"I don't know why you think I should help you. You're a gulag-bound criminal illegally loose on planet Earth. They aren't going to let you free."

"I have you to help me with that."

"I'm not helping you."

"Oh, but they will. You're the only sister in your family and the youngest." He grinned with certainty that he was accurate. Valene didn't know how he knew so much about her, but suspected Daphne Charlene had something to do with it. Or perhaps he'd been given the information on Alpha-Prime before leaving. His ability to fog the minds of Alphas had likely given him all sorts of advantages over the years.

Valene dropped her head. He also had a point. Her brothers might do any number of things to ensure she was returned to them safely. "You'll be free as soon as your brother brings me what I want."

"Even so, Royal Magistrate Guardsmen will spend the rest of eternity hunting you down until you're caught."

He grinned. "Let them try. This planet is a wonder. Around every corner is a new hiding place and with my singular skills I'm not worried at all. I knew if I could get to Earth, I'd find a way to be free forever. This planet is spectacularly more perfect than I envisioned."

Indigo opened the door. Valene yanked free of his hold and ran down a hallway toward the sound of a television. Maybe someone was here who could help her.

"Help!" Valene heard Indigo gaining on her as she took a sharp right-hand turn into a large area like a living room. Two people, an older man and woman, sat on a sofa watching a large flat-screen television.

"Help!" Neither of them even looked in Valene's direction. The television show looked like a war movie and the sound was turned up rather loud.

"Help me!" she screamed again, making it into their field of view. They looked stoned. Wait. Were they even alive? She screamed again at the thought that he'd killed these poor old folks.

"Stop screaming." Indigo put a hand over her mouth and whispered in her ear, "Settle down."

"Did you kill them? Are they dead?"

"No. They are simply under my spell. For some reason you became immune after the first time I used my unique power on you. I still don't know why."

Valene straightened. She frowned and turned to him. "I don't know what you have planned, but I will fight you every step of the way. You kidnapped me. Why would I help you?"

"Because if you don't, these folks are expendable."

"No."

"You're lucky I'm out of shackle stickers, Valene, or else I'd slap one on you again and make my permanent escape so much easier." Ah-ha! She'd been shackled to bend her to his whims. That made sense. At least she hadn't fallen for his charms. Had she?

"Permanent escape? How do you expect to do that?"

"No comment. Just because you are a part of my genius plan doesn't mean I will let you in on all the specifics."

"Genius plan?" Valene almost scoffed, but thought better of it. She was the one in handcuffs, not him. Maybe she should go along and try to thwart him later. That would be the smart plan.

"That's right. I'm so much smarter than everyone I meet. A burden I alone must bear, but I figure that living the rest of my life here on Earth will be much easier than on Alpha-Prime and certainly a large step up from the most notorious gulag in three galaxies."

"You're really planning to stay on Earth?"

He opened his mouth as if to tell her, then paused. "You don't really want to know my plan, do you?"

Valene frowned. "Maybe. Why?"

"If you know my plan, then either you'll have to come with me willingly or I'll have to use my unique skill on you to make you forget." He snapped his fingers. "Wait. You're immune to my skill."

He stared at her. What might he do to keep her quiet? Maybe she didn't want to find out.

"Fine. Don't tell me. I don't want to know anyway." Valene planned to pretend indifference. She would look for an opportunity to ruin his carefully laid plans.

"Are you going to cooperate?"

"Depends on what you expect me to do."

"I expected you to be under my thrall. Quiet, obedient, pleasant."

Valene snorted at the word obedient, but shrugged. "I won't make a scene only because I don't want you to hurt anyone else."

"Good. I believe you. Now, let's go. We've got a stop to make along the way that will likely take much longer than I intended."

Valene resisted the urge to ask where they were going. As long as she wasn't ensconced in the car's trunk, she'd figure it out soon enough anyway.

The couple on the sofa never once looked up from the loud war movie.

"Are they going to be okay?"

"They'll be fine."

"Who are they?"

Indigo paused as if considering whether to share, then shrugged. "Daphne's parents. This is their place. I couldn't stay in Alienn, of course."

Of course. Valene looked around at the luxurious home. She didn't know Daphne Charlene came from money. She'd always heard about her *aw shucks, I was always so poor* past and her subsequent short-term vault to success in the restaurant business.

She owned Skeeter Bite's most popular place to eat. The formerly historic building had been completely revamped from a rundown dry goods store into Critter's Café. Valene had never eaten there, but lots of folks said it was very good.

Maybe her success had provided her parents with a nicer home in their retirement. Daphne Charlene's character went up a notch in Valene's mind.

Indigo led her up a short set of stairs from the finished basement into the garage, accessed from the hallway next to an elegant and top-notch gourmet kitchen. Nice.

As they stood next to a very expensive and new-looking silver SUV, Indigo removed the cuffs from behind Valene's back and promptly zip-tied one arm to the passenger seat hand grab. So annoying. The pungent new car scent rushed into her lungs as he got into the driver's seat.

He pushed the button on a remote and a garage door opened behind them. Without any difficulty or hesitation, he wheeled the vehicle backward out of the garage, clicked the remote to close the door and drove down a long driveway bordered by very tall trees.

"Earth is amazing. I certainly understand why this backwater colony planet is so popular."

Valene didn't comment. She just looked out the window, trying to be ready for anything.

"Is that why you don't want to marry that Wyatt guy and leave?"

She whipped her head around so fast it was a wonder she didn't hurt herself. "How do you know about that?"

Indigo gave her a superior smile. "Daphne shared quite a lot about you and him and how she wished you would drop dead so she could have him. I also heard about the sheriff's heartfelt proposal. The one you turned down in something called a biker bar, whatever that is. Daphne was particularly upset about that. But if it were me, I'd never want to leave here even for love."

The notch up Valene had given Daphne Charlene for how she treated her elderly parents fell back down again in light of the fact the woman wanted her to drop dead so she could have Wyatt. She turned back to her window view. "Doesn't matter why."

"He's human. You're not. If you married a human, you'd both have to go to Alpha-Prime. I'm trying to be on your side. I'm saying I understand why you'd never want to leave here."

Valene mentally rolled her eyes. "That's not why I turned him down."

"Oh? Why not then? Enlighten me."

She shrugged, unwilling to share her reasons with this man. "What difference does it make?"

"I like learning things about people."

Valene decided to get along. "It's because Wyatt wouldn't be able to tell his family. He'd just disappear and they'd never know what happened to him." If one arm hadn't been tied above her head, Valene would have crossed her arms and pouted.

"Interesting."

"Whatever."

"I mean, that's very civil of you, taking into consideration his family's feelings and pain in spite of your obvious affection for your human."

Indigo didn't say anything else. He seemed to be mulling over her decisions as they drove. They traveled along the main road to downtown Old Coot, Arkansas. If Old Coot's sheriff, Hunter Valero, saw her, he'd likely wonder why she was riding along with someone other than Wyatt. Would he stop them? Maybe.

Valene watched for Wyatt's best friend as they went from one end of town to the other, and tried to think of a clever plan to let him know she was in trouble. They didn't see a single other vehicle on the road. They finally turned onto a smaller street filled on either side with houses.

A left turn, a right, another right—Valene lost track of direction in the maze of the housing division where each house looked very much like its neighbor's. Valene went back to wishing Hunter had been out and about patrolling, but apparently he was otherwise occupied. Probably just as well, as she hadn't come up with any plan to alert him that she was in trouble.

Another turn to the right put them in a more upscale sub-division where the houses weren't as cookie-cutter as the previous neighborhood.

Indigo turned into the driveway of a very nice home with a three-car garage, a rarity in this area. He picked up a different remote and pushed a button. The middle garage door opened and he pulled the big SUV in like he did it every single day. He turned the vehicle off and got out, closing the garage door with the remote as he rounded the front bumper to her side of the vehicle.

"Where are we?" Valene asked.

"Don't you already know?" He asked the question like he had a trick up his sleeve that she hadn't figured out yet and was amused by her ignorance.

"No idea."

"Well, it will be a surprise then." He zip-tied her hands in front of her and pointed to the door leading into the house. When she didn't move, he dragged her by her wrists toward it.

Inside the house, there was a short hallway going only one way. Indigo pushed her back against the wall. "You should stay here," he said, walking a couple of steps toward what looked like the entrance to the kitchen. "I can't be responsible for your feelings if you follow me." He grinned. What was he up to?

Valene could see the corner of the refrigerator. His expression dared her to follow him. She lifted away from the wall, eyes narrowing, and wondered what he was up to.

In the doorway, his back to her, Indigo stood stock still for a couple of seconds and then morphed before her eyes into the man she was in love with, Wyatt.

From the top of his head to the crisply pressed sheriff's uniform he always wore to his well-worn dark brown boots. She gaped.

How did Indigo do that? How was he an Alpha shapeshifter? How had he turned into Wyatt?

Indigo grinned at her with Wyatt's sweet mouth as *she* stared at him in horror, suddenly realizing the scope of his incredible powers. No wonder he'd been able to escape from any prison anywhere.

"Daphne," he called out using Wyatt's voice. "Where are you, darlin'? It's me, Wyatt."

Valene's mouth dropped open in utter shock.

What fresh space potato hell is this?

"Wyatt?" Daphne Charlene's very surprised voice came from the kitchen. Indigo-Wyatt disappeared into the kitchen.

Valene moved slowly forward, unable to stop herself from walking to the doorway to see what he planned to do.

Indigo-Wyatt winked at Valene and then kissed a happily shocked Daphne Charlene passionately on the mouth.

Road Trip to Suspicion, Minnesota

Dixie Lou dug up the address of the dead woman she planned to visit before leaving home—well, alleged dead woman. This would be an epic journey and exciting mission to discover why Constance Brickwood had faked her death. She couldn't wait to get the juicy details.

She plugged the Minnesota address into the fancy navigation system of the vehicle she'd borrowed from her boyfriend, Ed, gathered a few supplies and hit the road with Miss Penny.

"How long will it take us to get there?" her friend asked as they passed the final Maxwell the Martian billboard on the northbound road out of Alienn.

"A day and a half, if we hit it hard. Two if we take our sweet time."

"Do you know how long we'll be there?"

"Not sure yet. We'll have to figure it out as we go along. Why? Do you have an important appointment coming up or something? Do you have to be back in Alienn by a certain time?"

"Oh no, not really. But Ellie Mae Foster is having her open house and garden party in two weeks, remember? You and I had decided to attend to see if she spent too much money redecorating her home to look like one of those crazy makeovers that no one in their right mind would ever want to live in."

"Ooh, that's right. I forgot in all the excitement. We do not want to miss that. Let's hit it hard and try to make it there in a day and a half. We'll both take turns driving." She pressed the gas pedal down, automatically looking around for any police vehicles that might catch her speeding.

Dixie Lou smiled. She hadn't talked her way out of a traffic ticket in quite a long time.

Chapter 15

Wyatt found a perfect location to set up his gun stand at the bauxite pit's lovers' lane. There was a strategically located picnic table inside the edge of the woods just out of sight to anyone driving by. One end was half buried in the dirt after the area flooded a few years back, moving the wooden table from the eating area by a pavilion and depositing it here. No one had bothered to dig it up and move it back.

The angle and location were perfect for him to flatten onto his stomach across the length of it and rest his alien purple goo splatter gun barrel between two chipped plank ends of the tabletop's edge.

Looking through the newly attached riflescope, he was in place to get a great shot at Mr. Flirty. He couldn't wait. Through the line of trees at the edge of the road and across the shallow ditch, Diesel, Cam and Axel waited for the infamous Alpha criminal to come and trade Valene for whatever he wanted. Wyatt wasn't completely sure what that was.

They initially assumed it was the ID and the reverse Defender, although Wyatt didn't expect them to hand over either of those items. Wyatt planned to take his shot before they ever got to the trading part. Once he saw Valene was safe and had a shot that wouldn't come near her, he'd take it.

The other interesting part of this ingenious and intricate criminal plot involved a bunch of gold ingots currently residing in five prisoner cryo-pods aboard the gulag ship. No one knew how Indigo—what a stupid name—planned to get all those stacked gold ingots out of the pods. Diesel reasoned that maybe the ingots were unrelated and completely separate from Indigo's escape plan. Was a guard involved in this interesting turn of events? Was the gold something not included with the alleged genius criminal's escape plans? Somehow Wyatt doubted it.

More likely it was how Indigo planned to finance his whirlwind trip across Earth. They'd spent the whole evening shooting down various plans, but the only thing Wyatt cared about was getting Valene back safely.

Diesel agreed, but he wanted to ensure Indigo was captured, knocked out and stuffed back into his cryo-pod headed out of the galaxy tomorrow morning as planned. Whatever it took.

A car approached. In the earbud specially fixed for this meeting, he heard Diesel say, "Get ready, everyone."

Wyatt peered through his scope, trying to get a look at who was driving. As the vehicle got closer, he got a surprise.

In his ear, someone said, "Is anyone else seeing what I'm seeing?"

"I see her," Wyatt said. "Daphne Charlene is driving and Valene is right beside her. I don't see Indigo, but maybe he's hunkered down in the back seat or stuffed in the trunk, waiting to make his move somewhere down the road."

The vehicle stopped and Daphne Charlene jumped out of the driver's seat, rounding the front of the car to the passenger side where Valene remained seated.

Wyatt was relieved to see her, but Valene's expression looked dang near demonic. He'd never seen her display such a fierce frown. Daphne Charlene pulled Valene out of the car, forcing her to stumble to keep her balance. The frown worsened. Daphne Charlene pulled a gun out of her jacket pocket and pointed it at Valene's side.

"Don't do anything stupid!" she said harshly, slamming the door closed with one foot. "I don't want to accidentally kill your sister."

Daphne Charlene grabbed a still wobbly-footed Valene and put the gun barrel to her head.

Wyatt focused his attention on Valene. He'd been grateful to see her alive when they drove in.

He'd never seen such a harsh expression on her face, not even when she was at her angriest. Then again, the worst frown he'd ever seen before today had also been in the presence of Daphne Charlene.

Valene's hands were zip-tied in front of her. She scowled when the other woman pushed her toward Diesel, who waited ten feet away next to his large SUV.

The love of Wyatt's life fairly sneered as she was pushed along. He figured she had every right to. Not only was Daphne Charlene here, a crazed criminal had kidnapped her. She had a right to look her angriest.

He looked around at the forest edge and along the path their vehicle had come from, searching for the third party in this exchange. Unfortunately, Wyatt didn't have a target yet. Where was Indigo Smith?

"I don't see Indigo anywhere. He must be well hidden. Now what?" Wyatt whispered. "Want me to shoot Daphne Charlene?"

Diesel shook his head slightly, not taking his eyes off Valene.

Daphne Charlene said, "Whoever is out in the woods ready to shoot Indigo better just come out. He knows you set someone up. He won't show himself until he feels safe."

Diesel made a slashing motion across his throat, signaling that Bubba and Luther—also hidden strategically out in the woods—were to come out. Both of them did, hands half in the air, guns slung loose over their shoulders.

Wyatt stayed in place. He surveyed the area, looking for Indigo or any movement along the road or hidden in the woods along the roadway. Nothing.

He went back to watching Valene. He could only see the back of her head. She stood five feet from Diesel. As soon as she was free, he planned to tell her he was ready and willing to do whatever it took, even move to an alien planet to ensure they spent the rest of their lives together.

Valene's back was rigid. She had the air of an innocent party forced to participate in something unseemly against her will. That was the truth.

"Where is Wyatt?" Daphne Charlene asked, searching the area.

"Wyatt?" Diesel cocked his head to one side. "Why would he be here?"

Daphne Charlene jammed the gun into Valene's temple and screamed at the top of her lungs, "Where is Wyatt?"

"Where do you think he is?" Diesel asked.

"I think he's in the woods somewhere waiting to shoot Indigo. Make him come out." She looked around the area, focused her attention briefly on the car they'd driven to the rendezvous in and then turned her sharp gaze back to Diesel.

Wyatt saw Diesel's defeated expression. "I'm on my way," Wyatt whispered, noting Diesel looked only marginally relieved. He wasn't going to exit the woods here. He'd circle around and enter the area behind Diesel.

In his earpiece, he heard Diesel push out a long breath and say, "He's on his way."

Wyatt slung his alien purple goo splatter gun over one shoulder and made his way silently through the woods. Even Bubba and Luther looked surprised when he appeared next to them, moving past their resolute, ready-to-fight postures.

Wyatt crept in quietly behind Diesel and the assembled group, still in standard confrontation mode.

Daphne Charlene smiled. "There you are, Wyatt."

Valene looked less happy to see him, her gaze dropping to the ground between them, but she'd been through a lot and had a gun to her head. He understood her unease.

"Where is Indigo Smith?" Diesel asked.

"He's close," Daphne Charlene said, pushing the barrel of the gun into Valene's head a little harder. Wyatt's fists clenched and he had to forcibly open them. *Relax.*

"Here's what's going to happen," Daphne Charlene said, looking over one shoulder at the car they'd come in. "Wyatt, Valene and I are going to leave with what we came for and then—"

"Not a chance," Diesel interrupted her.

"What?" Daphne Charlene looked stunned and perturbed.

"We make the trade, Valene stays here and then you leave."

Daphne Charlene's eyes narrowed. "Fine. Hand it over."

"Hand what over? The ID, the reverse Defender gun, what?"

She looked smug. "Indigo said you wouldn't be smart enough to figure out his genius plan."

"Which doesn't help him, does it?" Diesel laughed. "What does Indigo Smith want in exchange for our sister?"

"All he wants is the item he accidentally left behind in his cryo-pod before escaping."

Diesel reached into his pocket and pulled out a dark gunmetal-colored box. It was the size of a deck of playing cards, but twice as thick. Wyatt had no idea what the item was or how long the brothers Grey had been in possession of it. Maybe they *were* smart enough to figure out the criminal alien's plan.

Valene smiled at her brother. "I knew you'd find it, Diesel," she said. The hard edge of her tone surprised Wyatt.

He stared at her. She met his gaze, but lost the smile. Was she still upset with him? Usually, when she looked at him it was with some sort of awe-inspired gratitude, like she never expected to find someone to fall in love with and staring at him reminded her that they loved each other. Right now, not so much.

Wyatt glanced at Daphne Charlene, who looked like she was about to have a meltdown. His other worry had to do with what she'd been telling Valene. Did she think he'd been with Daphne Charlene that night in the kitchen? He was almost afraid to find out. He'd have to work extra hard to ensure Valene knew that Daphne Charlene was a liar. Was now the time to clear things up? Probably not.

An indistinct thud from the direction of the car startled most of the assembled folks. Who was in the trunk of the car? A light bulb went off in Wyatt's head.

"Are you still mad at me, Valene?" Wyatt asked in an elevated tone. Everyone looked at him.

Her brows narrowed. "Why would I be?"

Wyatt shrugged. "You just don't seem like yourself, that's all. Daphne Charlene lied to you if she insisted we were together in my kitchen. It's not true."

Daphne Charlene's eyes widened. She looked ready to crack, but she held it together.

Valene's unbending stance went even more rigid. "I've had a difficult time recently, as if you couldn't tell." Her gaze left his and landed on Daphne Charlene before she fixed her gaze back on Wyatt.

Wyatt nodded. "True. Still, I need to tell you something. I'm willing to move to Alpha-Prime." He heard another thump from what sounded like the trunk of the car.

Valene tilted her head to one side. He'd never

seen her do that before. "Won't you miss your family?"

"Does a bear poop in the woods?"

Valene frowned. "What? Why is *that* relevant?"

Wyatt flipped his alien purple goo splatter gun up and shot Valene in the collarbone. Purple goo splattered down her chest and up her throat and chin, with a few healthy-sized spots landing on her cheeks.

She dropped to the ground, a stunned expression frozen in place. Diesel grabbed his rifle barrel, pointed it to the night sky and put a meaty hand around Wyatt's arm. He gave Wyatt a withering look that said vengeance would be his next reality.

Before anyone could retaliate, Valene's body began to writhe and change. Everyone stared as Valene morphed into...someone else. Daphne Charlene jumped away, but Bubba Thorne grabbed her and kept her from escaping. "He made me do it!" she screamed. "He made me help him. Now I get to have Wyatt." Her arms reached for Wyatt, but he backed up a step. Diesel released him as he watched fake Valene. Wyatt's gaze moved to the trunk of the car. Another thump came along with a muffled feminine screech of unhappiness. Wyatt's feet were moving toward the car before his brain caught up. No one stopped him.

On the ground, Valene was no longer Valene, but a subdued Indigo Smith dressed as Valene.

"How did you know?" Diesel asked behind him. Wyatt didn't have time to answer. He slung the rifle over his shoulder and reached inside the open passenger door to retrieve the key fob. He popped the trunk lock as he ran around to find the real Valene trussed up like a Thanksgiving turkey.

Wyatt whipped out his pocketknife and cut the rope at her ankles and wrists, carefully pulling the tight handkerchief from between her lips. "There you are." He helped her out of the trunk, hugging her tight the moment she was on her feet.

"How did you know it was Indigo and not me?" she asked, her voice muffled against his chest.

He drew back a little, but refused to let her get too far away. He grinned at her sweet face. She had that look again. The awe-inspired one. The one he loved without reason.

"Lots of things. I noticed you weren't wearing my ring."

Valene lifted her hand. "I still have it."

Wyatt smiled with gratitude. "Also, right up front he had a sneering frown that I've never seen on you before, even after being kidnapped and everything. But the true test was when I asked him, 'Does a bear poop in the woods?'" Even as bedraggled as she looked and after all she'd been through, Valene giggled.

"He didn't giggle like you just did. He said, 'What?' and asked me why *that* was relevant. You *always* giggle." Wyatt hugged her tight. Best of all, she hugged him back. "So I shot him in the collarbone. If he'd been wearing his own face, I would have shot him in the teeth, but…" Wyatt shrugged. "I just couldn't shoot yours."

"That's so sweet."

Wyatt suddenly remembered something he needed her to know. "I swear to you that I didn't do anything with Daphne Charlene in my kitchen that night."

"I know. I'm sorry you saw me with Indigo Smith. He put a shackle sticker on me."

Before he could comment, Diesel appeared at their side like magic. They parted, but Wyatt kept an arm around her shoulder.

"I thought you'd lost your mind for a minute there. Glad you figured it out when you did," Diesel said to Wyatt with a sheepish look.

"Trust me, it was my pleasure to land a purple goo pellet on Indigo."

Diesel pulled Valene away from Wyatt to give her a relieved brotherly hug. "I was worried about you." He leaned back to look into her eyes. "I'll bet you have quite a story to tell."

"You got that right," she said. "Indigo Smith is an Alpha shapeshifter."

Looking at Wyatt, Diesel said, "Luckily, Wyatt here figured that out before we made a foolish mistake."

"What's in that metal box that Indigo wanted?" Wyatt asked. "And where did you get it?"

Diesel held out the box, which upon closer inspection Wyatt saw had a button slide opening. Inside was a complicated-looking device.

"Wow. That's colorful. What does it do?"

"It is a remote control that opens up pre-programmed outer doors beneath certain cryo-doors on the prisoner ship. Axel found it when they did a thorough search on board the gulag ship earlier."

"The ingots," Wyatt said.

Diesel nodded. "Yep. As near as we can figure, he planned to jettison the five special pods that carried the ingots onto the ground and hide in the nearby forest as the ship took off for the gulag. Originally, his was the only pod that was set to open. The solar flares that opened all the rest of the pods ruined his carefully laid plans."

"Amazing."

Diesel shook his head. "It's ingenious. He had a complex plan to escape, hang around in town until the ship left and jettison the five pods of gold ingots into the safety of the woods. That gold is pure, too, and way more valuable here on Earth than on Alpha-Prime."

"How did he plan to transport the ingots? Five cryo-pods full sounds heavy."

"We don't know yet. We'll have to interrogate him."

Valene perked up. "I think I know."

"What do you know?" Diesel asked.

"Daphne Charlene gave him a key. It was an old rusty one, like an oversized skeleton key."

"What does it unlock?"

"Get this. Daphne Charlene has a secret tunnel beneath Critter's Café that leads out into the woods. She said the tunnel was built during Prohibition for customers to escape the old speakeasy in the basement if the police raided them."

"Interesting."

"I believe he planned to store the gold there until he could get a large enough vehicle to transport the ingots out of Arkansas. He was right. With his ability to change form, it would have been very difficult for even the Royal Magistrate Guard to track him down here on Earth."

"Amazing. I'll bet you're absolutely right. Let's head back to the basement conference room for a full debrief. We'll get Indigo back into his cryo-pod and take extra care to keep him subdued before the gulag ship takes off tomorrow morning."

"Great idea." Valene looked at the convict stretching out one of her favorite outfits. "Also, burn those clothes he's got on. Since I already saw him morph into someone else, complete with clothes, the only reason he wanted mine was to have some fun with me." She looked down at what she was wearing. Instead of one of Daphne Charlene's outfits, Indigo had insisted she wear his.

"I want to get back to the truck stop and change out of these prisoner clothes, okay?"

"No problem. But for the record, you look great in anything you wear."

"Spoken like a true fiancé," Diesel said with a smile. Wyatt's heart lifted. He hoped Diesel's words meant he wasn't bound for a permanent memory erasure. Maybe he could be trusted to keep their secret, and his relationship with Valene. He'd discuss it with Diesel once they got back to the truck stop.

Valene put her hand in his and they linked fingers as they walked toward the assembled group surrounding a purple-splattered, very subdued Indigo. Wyatt's heart flipped over the simple gesture of holding hands with his girl. He never wanted to be without her ever again. He planned to propose for a third time as soon as possible.

Daphne Charlene, still held in check by Bubba, gave them a scornful look as they passed by. Valene stopped and turned into him, kissing his mouth like they were alone in his bedroom.

Beside them, Daphne Charlene made an evil hissing noise and elbowed Bubba hard enough to make him grunt. Valene pulled away and stared into Wyatt's eyes with what looked like equal parts wonder and regret, but didn't acknowledge Bubba or Daphne Charlene's subsequent struggle in the wake of the wondrous kiss.

Wyatt only had eyes for Valene. Bubba could fend for himself. And if he had to leave Earth, Wyatt couldn't wait to tell her about his decision to move to her planet so they could spend the rest of their lives together.

Chapter 16

Valene changed clothes and took a quick refreshing shower in one of the basement guest rooms set aside for traveling dignitaries or VIPs who didn't want to remain aboard whatever ship brought them to Earth.

Her limited clothing options from the lost and found box included a lime-green Maxwell the Martian T-Shirt two sizes too big and black sweatpants one size too small. She looked like she was headed to a galactic yoga class. There were worse looks—for example, dirty, ripped men's prison clothing from an escaped criminal mastermind aided by her worst nemesis.

She towel-dried her hair then finger combed and fluffed her bangs as best as she could before putting the whole damp mess into a ponytail. She shook her head, decided it was at least a step up, and exited the bathroom into the main room of the VIP quarters.

Wyatt insisted on waiting for her before they both headed to the conference room for what

Diesel called the *we are lucky this turned out so well* debrief. He stood up the moment she entered the room, took one look at her outfit and a wide grin shaped his luscious mouth.

"Don't even say it."

"What?"

"This outfit is atrocious."

"It's not that bad. I really like the tight black sweatpants."

"You would."

Valene studied Wyatt, grateful he hadn't run screaming the first time they brought him into the basement area. She loved him so much and wanted to spend the rest of her life with him, but simply couldn't take him from his family. Her decision was made. Final answer.

Seeing Daphne Charlene's parents drugged while watching television like they had no life left in them made her think that's what Wyatt's parents would look like if she took him from them forever. She couldn't do it. She just couldn't make others miserable for her own happiness.

Valene planned to discuss her decision with Gage before the meeting so he could prepare the memory wipe. This debrief meeting would be her last time together with Wyatt. Glancing at the clock on the wall, she sped her pace. "We'd better get going, we don't want to be late."

"After the meeting, we're going to have a serious discussion about our future, okay?"

Valene nodded. "Yes. We definitely are." *Unfortunately, you'll have to forget all about me. But I'll never forget you.*

Hand in hand, fingers twined, they made their way to the conference room. She pointed to two chairs at the end of the table and told Wyatt to snag them while she talked to Gage. He kissed her cheek and did what she asked.

Sidling up next to her brother, she said in a near whisper, "Gage, I need you to set up a memory wipe for Wyatt. I need it to go back a year. Before we met."

"What?"

The shock in his tone surprised her, but Valene was resolute. "You heard me."

"I thought he wanted to marry you."

"He does, but I can't let his family suffer. I just can't. I can't be happy at his family's expense." Her eyes filled with unshed tears. "Please."

"Have you talked to Wyatt about it?"

"No."

"You should."

"I can't. I don't want him to talk me out of it."

"You should still discuss it with him, Valene. He obviously loves you."

"And I love him, but it doesn't matter. This is the way it has to be. Please, Gage."

Gage looked unhappy, but after a few seconds he nodded. "I'll have to get Cam to help me, but I'll get it set up."

"Thank you." Valene breathed a sigh of relief, vowing to let her emotional girly-girl side have a good cry later. For now, she'd spend her last few minutes with Wyatt, soak up his warmth and then say her final good-bye.

Skeeter Bite, Arkansas Sheriff's Office, two weeks later

Diesel pulled his SUV into a wide space in the parking lot behind the sheriff's office and killed the engine. It wasn't that he cared if anyone saw them here, but he didn't want to call attention to them in case things didn't go according to plan.

"Do you think Wyatt is okay?" he asked his brother.

Cam shrugged. "I don't know. That's what we're here to discover, right?" He reached for his door to get out.

"Yep," Diesel replied, but remained seated. "I heard his family put him in the hospital for several days after Hunter Valero found him unconscious at his home."

"They only did it as a precaution because he had such a terrible headache. Hunter told me he got out of there as soon as he could."

"Still, his pain was because of our procedure." The news of Wyatt's painful memory erasure upset

Diesel. Valene was nearly inconsolable when she heard.

"I know. It's unusual. No one has ever exhibited that symptom before. Gage is looking into it."

"What's he doing?"

Cam shook his head. "Pfft. I have no idea. Science-y Gage stuff like usual. You know how he is."

Diesel knew Gage was almost more upset by the side effects than Valene had been. "He just didn't expect Wyatt to have such a hangover after the memory wipe.

Someone passed in front of their vehicle, swiped an access card at the back door and entered the rear entrance of the Skeeter Bite Sheriff's Office. Diesel and Cam would have to go around to the front.

"We should get inside and check Wyatt before too many more people show up."

Diesel opened his door. "Let's hope he's blissfully ignorant of what we did to him. Plus, I'd hate to see him like Valene."

"That's the truth. She is one miserable chickadee since Wyatt lost his memory about us."

Diesel cracked a smile. "She hates it when you call her a chickadee."

Cam grinned. "I know. That's why I do it. Come on, let's get this over with."

They exited Diesel's vehicle into a warm and very humid day and quickly made their way to the front door, stepping into air-conditioned bliss inside the station. The receptionist recognized them and waved them back to Wyatt's office at the rear of the building.

"Hey, Diesel." He stood and extended his arm to shake hands. "Cam," he added and shook his hand as well. "What brings you boys to Skeeter Bite?"

Diesel and Cam sat in the chairs stationed in front of Wyatt's desk. "We heard you'd come back to work today and wanted to check up on you. Heard you spent some time in hospital after some sort of head injury."

"That's nice of you. I appreciate it."

Cam leaned forward and looked carefully into Wyatt's face. "So, how are you? What do you remember about your…accident?"

Wyatt's smile dimmed. "I don't remember what happened that knocked me unconscious in my own yard, but Hunter suspects I got hit by a loose limb that fell on my head. He was the one who found me, along with one of my sisters."

"That's pretty scary," Diesel said, also studying Wyatt. He seemed okay.

"Well, I feel bad because technically it was scary for everyone except me. I don't remember a thing."

Cam seemed to relax back in his chair. "Maybe that's for the best."

"Only one drawback that I can see so far."

"What's that?" Diesel asked, also easing back in his chair.

"It seems that my lost memory has prompted

pretty much everyone I meet to let me know I owe them money. Turns out I'm in debt somewhere in the neighborhood of three years' worth of salary. Makes me wonder what I was spending all that borrowed money on."

Diesel and Cam both laughed.

"Oh, yeah, lots of knee-slapping fun on that score."

"I'll bet," Diesel said.

"Good news, Wyatt," Cam said. "We truly only came to check on you, not turn you upside down and shake any coins loose to collect on imaginary debts."

"That *is* good news."

"Beyond all that money you owe, do you remember anything useful?"

"The last thing I remember was going into a restaurant for lunch almost a year ago. Then, poof, nothing. In the past couple of weeks, I've recalled a few images where I'm hunting in nearby woods, but I used to do that almost every weekend and have since I was a little kid here in Skeeter Bite. I might just be remembering trips from before a year ago." He shrugged, seemingly unconcerned about losing his memory. That was sort of a relief.

"My folks and especially my four sisters have caught me up on a year's worth of gossip regarding everyone in a three-county area. That's super fun." He paused, then added, "No, not really. I'm lying." He grinned and shook his head.

"What do your doctors say about the memory loss?"

Wyatt shrugged. "They don't know. Every doctor I talk to has a different theory. I figure I'm healthy enough for my purposes. The headache's gone and whether I remember the past year or not, I expect life will carry on like it did before."

Diesel nodded. "That's a good way to think about things." His phone buzzed in his pocket, signaling a text. He looked at the screen. A 9-1-1 message from Aunt Dixie. Heaven help him, even though she'd been on a trip for nearly two weeks, he still didn't feel like dealing with any of her shenanigans.

Wyatt laughed. "I just have to figure out a way to pay back all that money I owe."

Before Diesel or Cam could comment, Wyatt's receptionist came to the open door and leaned her head in to let the sheriff know there was someone to see him.

Cam stood up. "We'll get out of your hair, Wyatt. Good to see you and hear that you're on the mend."

Wyatt came around his desk and shook their hands again. "Thanks for stopping by. It was good to see you both."

Diesel looked out the window at his vehicle. "Could we slip out the back door? We're parked right there."

"Sure. It's around the corner and down the hallway." Wyatt turned to his receptionist and asked, "Who is here to see me? I don't have any appointments today, do I?"

"No, sir, you don't have any appointments today. This woman said she just wanted to stop in and say hi." The receptionist looked at Diesel and Cam for a long spell and added, "She said her name is Valene Grey."

"Your sister is here?" Wyatt looked at them, eyes scrunching in confusion. "That's strange. I wonder why."

Oh, I know exactly why. The phone in his pocket buzzed yet again. It was another text from Aunt Dixie, telling him she needed to see him pronto about some earth-shattering news. Which didn't move him, as that was what she always said about everything they discussed. From a price increase on any product at the local grocery store to every single money-making plan she told him about for the old folks' home, it was all an emergency.

Space potatoes.

Chapter 17

Valene was not supposed to be here. She had sworn on her life she would stay away from Wyatt after his memory wipe. She was playing with fire. No, she was playing with a glob of lava.

She paced in front of the reception desk, trying to decide whether to run out before he showed up or keep playing with the melted rock.

Valene kept playing. She had to see Wyatt with her own eyes. She had to know he was okay. If he was as interested as he was last time they met for the first time and asked her out, she'd say no and invent a fake boyfriend.

If any of her brothers found out about this little foray into Skeeter Bite to visit the sheriff, they'd probably blow a gasket. Even so, she needed to see him with her own eyes. Needed to assure herself he was okay. Needed to see him one last time. She pushed out a mental sigh. She was lying to herself.

This was such a bad idea. Valene turned to leave. Her hand touched the doorknob the same instant Wyatt said, "Hello. Valene, is it?"

She spun around and saw Wyatt, followed closely by a perturbed-looking Diesel and an equally unhappy Cam.

Valene stuck out her hand as if introducing herself. Wyatt took it, but seemed puzzled. She looked deeply into his eyes, but his expression remained quizzical.

"What can I do for you?" he asked politely. *Oh my. You can do so much. Stop it.* He gestured over his shoulder with a thumb. "Your brothers were kind enough to stop by and check out my auspicious return to work after my accident. I'm sorry, but if we've met in the last year…I forgot." There was a terrible silence for what seemed like forever before Wyatt cracked a smile and laughed.

He was making a joke. He didn't know her. He didn't remember them being together.

She was both relieved and devastated. Valene also laughed, but it was forced and had the dual function of keeping her from wailing in despair over the loss of Wyatt's love with his year-long memory wipe. She was in trouble and now she'd confirmed the fact he didn't wake up two weeks ago and remember a single thing about her. If he had, he would have tracked her down.

Diesel rolled his eyes behind Wyatt's back and moved toward her. Time was up. She was about to pay the piper for her foolish field trip.

"Let's not take up any more of the sheriff's time, Valene. We need to let the man get back to work."

"Right," she said as Diesel took her arm and pulled her a couple of steps toward the door. Cam grabbed her other arm and pushed her toward the door, too.

"Nice to meet you," Wyatt said.

"Likewise," Valene said, her eyes foolishly filling with unshed tears. They'd be falling just as soon as she got out of Wyatt's presence.

Her brothers pushed and pulled her toward the front door. Wyatt stepped closer, looked deeply into her eyes and said in a low tone, "Hope to see you again soon, Vee."

Valene stiffened, resisting the manhandling by her brothers. Wyatt snapped his mouth shut as if he suddenly realized he'd just made a horrible gaffe, but wasn't certain what he'd said that was so awful.

"Did you just call her Vee? Why would you do that?" Cam asked. He stopped pulling on Valene's arm. Diesel stopped pushing.

The receptionist walked back into the room, but no one said another word.

Wyatt glanced over one shoulder as the receptionist seated herself at her desk. He gave the three Grey siblings a rather sheepish look that said he remembered everything. How was that possible?

"Let me walk you outside," Wyatt said.

Diesel and Cam released Valene, but spun her around to head out the door frontward facing instead of being dragged out backward.

Out in the humid heat, Valene turned to face Wyatt. "You remember," she accused.

"Does a bear poop in the woods?" Valene giggled and leapt into his arms. He caught her and pushed his face into her throat, smelling her hair, kissing her cheek. "I've missed you so much, Vee."

"This is bad," Cam said. "This is really bad."

Diesel didn't say anything. He just cleared his throat several times until Valene let Wyatt go.

Wyatt put a finger up, opened the door and told his receptionist, "I'm going to go on patrol. I'll be back in a couple of hours or so."

"Sure thing, Sheriff."

He closed the door and turned to Diesel, putting his arm around Valene. "I assume Cam will be riding shotgun as usual, on the way to the basement of the Big Bang Truck Stop."

"You got that right." Cam looked like his mind had been blown. Maybe he was trying to figure out how Wyatt had gone through his invasive memory wipe program, but still had his memories. She wanted to know that, too. She also wanted to know what this meant for them. Would Wyatt be sent to Alpha-Prime? Would they experiment on him to discover why he was resistant to the memory wipe?

Gage was already trying to figure out why Wyatt had suffered such a terrible headache from the treatment.

Diesel didn't say anything as he climbed into the

driver's seat. When everyone else was inside, he drove all the way to Alienn without speaking a word. Cam asked a couple of questions, but Diesel remained silent.

Valene held hands with Wyatt all the way there, wondering what would happen next.

Once they were ensconced in the basement conference room behind locked doors, Diesel said, "Okay. Let's hear it. How do you remember?"

"I'm not sure how I remember." Wyatt shrugged. "When I woke up at my folks' house after being found unconscious, I remembered almost everything I'd learned about your Big Bang Truck Stop operation in the basement, but my head hurt so much that I spent a few days in the hospital. As the pain lessened, I remembered more. Now, I think I remember everything."

"Why didn't you contact us?" Cam asked.

"I wasn't sure what you'd do to me if the memory erase didn't work. I don't think you understand the gut-clenching pain of that headache. I pretended it was all a dream and didn't speak about it. By the time I was back home from the hospital, I remembered the whole year that was supposed to have been erased, not just the alien parts."

Diesel's phone buzzed. Aunt Dixie, with another urgent message, complete with lots of exclamation marks, demanding that he hurry his butt up and meet her in Gage's lab in the truck stop's basement.

Right now, Diesel! I mean it!! What was that woman up to?

Wyatt fidgeted like he was uneasy about his declaration. He eyed Valene more than once, making Diesel think about Juliana, his wife. She'd ultimately been immune to the Defender after a while because she had a touch of Alpha blood in her system.

His phone buzzed again. Aunt Dixie…again. *Are you on your way? Why not?*

"Who is sending you messages?" Cam asked. "The endless buzzing is making me want to hurl your cell phone far, far away."

"Aunt Dixie is back from her Lost Colony road trip adventure and wants to have a chat right now about all the things she learned. You know, because everything she's involved in is scare-me-speechless important."

"You'd better just bite the bullet and go talk to her, Diesel." Valene laughed when he made a face. "You know she won't stop until she hunts you down. Better just go get it over with."

"I don't think we are finished talking here yet."

Buzz. Buzz. Buzz.

Cam held his hand out with a look on his face that said he planned to destroy Diesel's phone with his bare hands. "Let me have it."

"Nope. I need my phone. I know. Let's all go to see Aunt Dixie together."

"What?"

"I say everyone gets to come with me and enjoy the show."

"That's mean." Cam stood anyway. "Where are we going?"

"Not far. Just Gage's lab."

As if his brother sensed he was being talked about, the next buzz was from Gage.

"Let me guess—Aunt Dixie again?" Cam asked sarcastically, moving toward the conference door.

"Nope. This time it's Gage. He says it really *is* important."

"Him I believe," Valene said. "We'd better get there, pronto." She grabbed Wyatt's hand and they all headed for Gage's lab.

Valene didn't know exactly what they were in store for, but Wyatt remembering everything made her joyful that maybe somehow something would work out for them. The last time she talked to Aunt Dixie, she'd said she was on the case to find a solution for Valene to be with Wyatt. Maybe her aunt was about to be her salvation.

Chapter 18

Dixie Lou was so excited she was practically jumping up and down. It had taken nearly two weeks to track down and discover all the awesome information they'd found. Luckily, they'd been in her boyfriend Ed's RV. They found a nice RV park, paid in advance for ten days, knowing they had to get what they needed by then in order to get back to Alienn for the open house party. Besides, having a time limit always made things so much more exciting. They almost didn't get what they needed in time.

The three days they allowed for travel back home was extended by two days so she could prove all of her suppositions. It was great to be right all the time.

Miss Penny sat quietly at the table with Gage, watching him read the incredible information they'd found. After all they'd learned in Suspicion, she insisted, and Miss Penny agreed, on driving straight through from Minnesota for seventeen hours to get here and tell everyone. And to attend the open house garden party tonight. They weren't about to give that up.

The only problem was Diesel was somewhere away from the truck stop and wasn't answering her text messages. Drat that boy!

Gage was reading through all the paperwork and information she'd found. His eyes were as big as saucers and every so often he'd mumble, "Wow. I can't believe it." Then he'd turn another page, read it and repeat what he'd said.

After waiting the longest hour of her life, Diesel and Cam finally entered the lab, followed by Valene and her sheriff, Wyatt.

"Oh, good. I'm glad you brought Valene and her beau."

"What's this about, Aunt Dixie? And if you tell me you need to discuss a new plan to make more money for the old folks' home using Lost Colony information, I will break you in half."

"No need to be grumpy, Diesel. That's not why I called you here. Although that might be a genius idea one of these days." She made a mental note to consider what fund-raising could be generated by the Lost Colony Legend.

Gage stood up. "This is amazing, Diesel. You will not believe what she found in Minnesota."

"More aliens," Aunt Dixie said.

"What are you talking about?"

"There is a whole town filled with folks

descended from a member of that fateful Lost Colony Legend trip."

"Who? I thought everyone died."

"The guard that everyone thought was dead because he never came back to the landing site where Miss Penny and her mom waited? Well, he survived."

Diesel's eyes narrowed in the same way they always did when she came to him with a grand money-making scheme for the old folks' home. "If he survived, why didn't he go back to the landing site?"

Dixie Lou couldn't contain herself. It was the best story she'd ever heard. Like a TV movie, only better, because it was true.

"He had an accident, hit his head and lost his memory."

"What? I don't believe it." Diesel had another familiar look, the skeptical one. He'd mastered it.

"It's true. He made it almost to the location of the supplies, but got hit in the head by a falling rock slide during some bad weather and lost his memory. Someone found him, took him into Suspicion, Minnesota and nursed him back to health. He couldn't remember who he was so he made a life there as a wheat farmer named Delvin Miller, and then later he had a mill that ground wheat into flour. Isn't that amazing?"

"Amazing? Okay. Sure." Diesel was the opposite of amazed. He was wary. "Suspicion,

Minnesota. I remember that name." Diesel's gaze went up for a moment as if he tried to recall what he'd heard. "There were rumors of people with mind-reading skills or something seventy or eighty years ago. Didn't Alpha-Prime send a Guardsman there several decades ago to investigate?"

Dixie Lou rocked from one foot to the other, her speed increasing as she revealed the details of her investigation. "Yes. They did. Seventy-seven years ago. Her name was Constance Brickwood and she sent a report back that said the guard wasn't there and she couldn't locate the supplies sent ahead in the harsh terrain where they were supposed to have landed, which then closed down any further action there."

"Okay." Diesel's brow-furrowing scowl was back.

"Then do you know what happened, Diesel?"

"I'm certain you're about to tell me no matter what I say."

She gave him a scolding look, but he was right. Dixie Lou was fairly bursting to tell them all about what she'd discovered. "It's so exciting. Anyway, after Constance submitted her, well, interpretation of events regarding no Alpha activity, it was reported that she was accidentally killed. She had no family or friends on Alpha-Prime to return to anyway."

"That's too bad," Diesel said.

"But guess what?"

"What?" Diesel played her game. He didn't smile, exactly, but he didn't seem as unhappy as usual.

"She was laid to rest in Suspicion by a local minister instead of being sent back to Alpha-Prime."

"Interesting. I'm surprised they didn't send a Guardsmen contingent to retrieve her."

"Yes. But way back then, they weren't as careful as they are now. Progress, right? But I also looked up the Alpha history of that particular time period and they were definitely not as strict as nowadays. Plus, there was lots of brouhaha going on about alien contact and whether the program of colonization should be scrapped. The powers in charge finally decided to move forward, but in all the ruckus, Constance's Earth burial was forgotten or deemed unimportant."

"Right. So she died and was buried in Suspicion. Why is that relevant now?"

Dixie Lou grinned wide. "Because..." Dixie quickly looked around to ensure everyone was listening closely when she said dramatically, "Get this! Constance faked her death."

More than one person gasped.

"Faked her death? I don't believe it," Diesel said.

Dixie Lou's feet were practically dancing a jig by now. "I know. Isn't it awesome? I didn't believe it either. So that's why Miss Penny and I took a road trip up there to investigate. We spent almost two weeks on the trail of this Lost Colony investigation to learn the truth."

"Is that where you went? To track down information on the Lost Colony Legend in Minnesota?"

"Yep. Good thing I did, too. After scouring my scrapbooks for historical information, I remembered Constance."

"You remembered her?"

"She was sent to Suspicion, Minnesota on the day I was born. Isn't that cool?"

"Very cool," Diesel agreed.

"Anyway, I found her sad story about ten years later when I started clipping interesting stories about Earth and Colonization. Way back then Alphas coming to Earth was big news. When I moved to Earth, I brought all my scrapbooks with me. I had to dig the articles out of my attic from my bargain sea trunk.

"Anyway, then I looked on the internet machine for any recent information and found a picture of Constance in the local newspaper with her husband from two years before. They had been married for seventy-five years, and she still looked great. I thought she might have had some work done, because no one can look that good, right? But then again, Alpha genes are really awesome…"

"Anyway," Diesel prompted.

"Anyway, her husband was a grandson of Lukas Marek, the Guardsman who never returned from his surveillance trip, a.k.a. Delvin Miller. Miss Penny said the grandson, Lukas Marek the Third, a.k.a. Delvin Miller the Third, was the spitting image of his grandfather. And she would know."

There was silence in the room as everyone seemed to digest her fantastical information.

Wyatt cleared his throat, and said, "Both of my parents were born and raised in Suspicion, Minnesota. I was born there, too, but we moved here when I was a kid. I was too little to remember anything like psychics roaming around town. My mother's people are Millers."

Valene grinned at her. "Thank you, Aunt Dixie."

"Don't get too excited about this," Diesel said, throwing cold water on the possibilities like he always did on all of Dixie Lou's fabulous money-making ideas. "We don't know anything yet."

As if it were staged to provide the best timing in a drama, Gage's phone let out a loud bong, startling everyone in the room. "It's the notification of the test I ran on a sample of Wyatt's blood to see if he's part Alpha."

"You have my blood?"

"I usually take a sample from everyone who comes through my lab…for my research database."

"Is that legal?" Wyatt asked.

Gage shrugged. "No one has ever complained about it before."

"They might if they knew you were doing it."

"Typically, I only take samples of Alphas. But

when you took the beanbag in the belly for Diesel, I grabbed a sample. Besides, I don't share the information with many people, certainly not any humans."

Wyatt shook his head, but didn't seem too worried about his blood being tested by Alphas without his permission. "Okay. Whatever. What does the report on my blood say?"

"I don't know, I'll have to go look."

"Great. I'll go with you," Wyatt said and winked at Valene.

"I want to go, too." Valene clung to Wyatt's hand, their fingers still laced.

Dixie Lou moved closer to Gage. "I think I should get to go. I was the one who cracked this case wide open."

"What case?" Diesel wanted to know.

"The case where Valene gets to marry her sheriff because he's part Alpha, just like your wife Juliana."

Wyatt perked up. "If I'm part Alpha, I can marry Valene? And we can stay here in Arkansas? Is that true?" His sweet loving gaze was only for Valene. They stared at each other silently for several seconds, until Diesel broke the spell.

"I know. Let's *all* go to Gage's lab, shall we?" Diesel quickly headed for the conference room door with everyone trailing behind him.

Dixie Lou trouped along with them, then passed everyone, beating even Gage to his lab because her feet wanted to do a dance of joy.

This was only the first of what would surely be many exciting and interesting stories to come out about the Lost Colony Legend of Alpha-Prime and the secret Alpha psychics in Suspicion, Minnesota.

Valene squeezed Wyatt's fingers again and again as they walked to Gage's lab. Aunt Dixie practically sprinted that way. Amazing, given her age, which no one really knew until now because that was the only information she would never spill.

Wyatt pulled on her hand, letting the rest of the pack get some distance away.

"Does this mean what I think it does?" he asked in a low tone.

"If you have even the most minor sliver of Alpha blood, then we can stay here and have a life together. And I'm pretty sure that's true." A huge light bulb had gone off in her head when Aunt Dixie started explaining about going to Minnesota and what she'd discovered there.

"Why?"

"Because they did a memory wipe on you and it didn't work." She grinned. "I'm pretty sure you're about to be stuck with me forever. Are you scared?"

"Nope." He gripped her hand and a smile danced around his luscious mouth. "Not even a little."

"Do I get the ring back?"

"Does a bear poop in the woods?"

Valene giggled.

By the time they walked into Gage's lab, it was clear by the revelry inside that Wyatt was Alpha enough to marry her.

Gage read from a piece of paper. "Wyatt Campbell definitely has Alpha blood in his system, but it is a different type than Juliana's royal blood."

"I don't have royal blood? Bummer," Wyatt said with a laugh.

He pulled the engagement ring out of his pocket, slipped it on Valene's finger and asked, "Will you still marry me even though I don't have royal alien blood, but instead Suspicion, Minnesota Alpha farmer's blood?"

"Yes! I love you, Wyatt. Besides, instead of royal blood, you have Guardsman blood. It's perfect for you."

"I love you, Vee." He pressed his lips to hers in a sweet kiss that turned less sweet after a few seconds. They broke apart when Diesel put a hand on each of their shoulders.

"I'm happy for you both. There will still be a bunch of paperwork before you can be official."

"No worries. It's usually not worth it if there isn't a ton of paperwork involved."

"Obviously, I will do whatever I can to expedite this. However, I don't expect you'll be able to tell your parents or any of your family about Alphas, maybe ever. Will that be a problem?"

"Nope. Honestly, I doubt they'd believe it anyway."

"Hunter also can't ever know. I don't think I can stress to you the importance of this."

Wyatt nodded. "I understand. Don't worry." He glanced at a grinning Valene. "I'll do whatever it takes to make a life with Valene on Earth. No one needs to know anything."

Valene moved in for a kiss. He obliged her. This was the first hopeful kiss he'd shared with her since they met. This kiss began their forever.

Epilogue

Two months later...

Wyatt stared at Valene in wonder. In a short while, they were hosting a party at Wyatt and now also Valene's house to celebrate their elopement exactly one week ago. The moment the extensive paperwork came back from Alpha-Prime that they could marry and live on Earth, they'd hightailed it to the Justice of the Peace and said, "I do."

One week of wedded bliss assured him their life together would be amazing.

"I need to tell you something," Valene said, placing a vase of flowers in the center of their dining room table.

"That you love me? I already know."

Valene smiled. "I do love you, but this is something else. A surprise."

"I love surprises."

"I hope you love this one."

Wyatt held up his three-fingered scout salute.

"It's a good thing we got married last week

because I'm pregnant and now we won't have to explain to my brothers…as much."

"Pregnant? Explain, as much?" That sounded bad. "Are you saying that the very first time we were together…" He didn't finish the sentence. "Did you know before we got married?"

Valene made a face, which probably meant yes, she'd known from the day after they'd slept together.

"I wasn't absolutely certain, but I knew it was a distinct possibility."

"It was always a possibility."

"Her expression changed to one of distress. Are you upset?"

"No. I'm just surprised. I mean, I can't believe it." He grinned wide. "But make no mistake, I can't wait to be a dad."

Valene released a long, relieved-sounding breath. "Whew."

"But are you okay? I mean, do you feel okay?" He hugged her close as dual feelings of concern and fatherly pride circled inside. His parents were going to freak out with joy. This would be their first grandchild.

"I feel great. Although I don't expect that to last. A friend from school told me once that she hurled for a couple of months early on."

"Does anyone else know?"

Valene grinned. "Nope. I wanted to tell you first. That's not to say that Aunt Dixie and my mother haven't both been eyeing me like they suspect something."

"Are you going to tell them at the party tonight?"

Valene looked surprised. "I hadn't planned on it. Do you want me to?"

"Does a bear poop in the woods?"

Valene giggled. "I figured you'd want me to push the idea of a premature birth in about seven months."

"Oh no. Not at all. Best to get that news out when there are lots of guests and family here because then your brothers can't kill me with so many witnesses to deal with."

"Like I said, good that we are already married."

Wyatt kissed her hand right below the wedding set she wore and said, "Thank you for marrying me, Mrs. Campbell."

"You're welcome. Also, I love the sound of my new name."

"So do I."

Wyatt kissed her. Then he kissed her again. He would have gone in for thirds, but the doorbell rang and it was time to party. He hoped he would survive the night after her brothers learned they were about to be uncles.

Coming next:
Four Weddings and an Alien, Alienn, Arkansas 5

ALIENS ACTUALLY
A NOCTURNE FALLS UNIVERSE COLLECTION

Pilot. Guard. Prisoner… *Stowaway.*

All are crashed in the Georgia woods, lost on a world where aliens are the stuff of science fiction. And what if the locals are far from human themselves?

CLOSE ENCOUNTERS OF THE ALIEN KIND

Stella Grey's mission was simple: Locate the downed ship in the Georgia woods. Secure the prisoner. And keep the earthlings from learning that aliens live among them, namely in Alienn, Arkansas.

Prisoner, Draeken Phoenix, is also the dangerously delicious man she left behind on Alpha-Prime to start a new life on Earth.

INVASION OF THE ALIEN SNATCHERS

Riker Phoenix, the guard, has everything but the tantalizing woman who changed the course of his life.

Elise Midori ran a galaxy away to escape the man she loved, but could never have. But it wasn't far enough, thanks to a crash in Nocturne Falls, and a crazy Druid high priestess intent on claiming him as her own.

THE ALIEN WHO FELL TO EARTH

Pilot, Holden Grigori is lost on an alien world, with no memory. A pretty woman claims she's his wife and loves him. He'd do anything for her.

Victoria Greene is sent to find the pilot and keep him safe as he recovers. Pretending to be his wife is not a hardship. Falling in love is even easier. But what happens when he gets his memories back and realizes that to him she is…no one.

More

Nocturne Falls Universe

Have Yourself a Merry Little Alien
Merry & Bright: A Christmas Anthology
(Nocturne Falls)

Draeken and Stella Phoenix are celebrating Christmas in Nocturne Falls with a festive holiday party in their new vacation home. Each has a big surprise for the other, but all's fair in love and secret Christmas presents. Right?

The Dragon's Spellbound Alien

Mind-reading Alpha-Prime alien Bianca Forrester leaps at the chance to work as a psychic in Nocturne Falls and rub shoulders with werewolves, gargoyles and fae in the Halloween-themed Georgia town. Not only will it be an adventure, it's the perfect place to dodge her mother's matrimony mania.

Half-human, half-dragon shifter Warrick Hart has never forgotten the fear and loathing he faced as a child in Europe when superstitious humans and human-hating supernaturals chased his family from town to town. It taught him to rely on no one but his mother and brother.

Bianca doesn't believe in love at first sight.

Warrick would never trust a woman with his heart.

But Nocturne Falls is a place where never becomes now and beliefs can change on a spell.

The Vampire's Unintended Alien

Isabel Winstead has found acceptance and excitement in the hidden alien community growing in Nocturne Falls, where werewolves and gargoyles and witches live in plain sight. She loves her life in the Halloween-themed Georgia town, loves her job and her friends and—sigh—loves an absolutely delicious and unattainable vampire who doesn't know she exists.

Half-vampire, half-sorcerer Viktor Hart revels in his bachelorhood. He adores his family, is a respected craftsman, drives a fast car and hangs out every night at Insomnia with his buddies. He's never met a woman he'd be willing to sacrifice his independence for. Until Isabel and one mind-blowing birthday kiss.

Naturally, it must be a love spell.

The honorable thing would be to break the spell and let Isabel make up her own mind—even if she doesn't choose him.

The Witch's Enchanted Alien

Paranormal private investigator and witch Ruby Hart needs a man—specifically, a man with a unique tattoo. Finding him for her anonymous client will put her fledgling business in the supernatural haven town of Nocturne Falls, Georgia in the black for months.

Maximilian Cornelius Vandervere the Fourth was a privileged and respected member of one of Alpha-Prime's most elite families before the Incident made him a social pariah. An uncomplicated life as Max Vander in the secret alien colony on Earth is the perfect solution.

The double whammy of a love spell and a truth spell is definitely a complication he doesn't need.

Ruby can't help but notice the tall, gorgeous blond alien. It's hard to ignore a man who keeps declaring his love and proposing marriage to a woman he's just met. And it's clear he needs help.

Sweet, sexy Max is a puzzle she can't resist.

YOU'VE GOT ALIENS
ALIENN, ARKANSAS 1

Librarian and aspiring journalist Juliana Masters has a mystery to solve: Who am I? Armed with the truth about her past, she can leave her humdrum present behind and get on with her future. She just needs to complete one lucrative investigative writing assignment and she'll be on her way. All she has to do is prove aliens live and work out of a secret facility based under the Big Bang Truck Stop. No problem. Getting her socks knocked off by the Fearless Leader isn't part of the plan.

Diesel Grey worked for years to achieve his goal of heading up the family business in Alienn, Arkansas. Mission accomplished, but being Fearless Leader of a galactic way station comes with a lot more headaches than anticipated. It's hard to consider the shockingly well-informed writer a headache, though, especially when she makes him ache in all the right places.

If he's not careful, he'll give her everything she needs to blow his family's cover and expose to the human world that aliens do walk among them.

All he really wants to do is sweep her up in his arms and never let her go.

AVAILABLE NOW

HOW TO LOSE AN ALIEN IN 10 DAYS
ALIENN, ARKANSAS 2

Alexandria Latham Borne is supposed to marry into one of Alpha-Prime's most prestigious families. Her unwanted future fiancé has wealth, breeding, social status...and that's about it. She is less than wowed during their luxury get-to-know-you journey to Earth. Once the spaceship docks in Alienn, Arkansas, Ria jumps at the chance to jump ship and explore the colony of extraterrestrials hiding in plain sight.

Cam Grey takes his job as chief of security at the galactic way station and the Big Bang Truck Stop operated by his family very seriously, but even he needs a break. No one suspects the by-the-book enforcer's secret refuge is the karaoke bar just over the county line from Alienn, Arkansas. It starts out as just another night of uncomplicated amusement. But no one is more surprised than the jaded Alpha when the gorgeous woman with blue-streaked hair sings her way into his bed — and his heart.

When he learns his sexy karaoke singer has defied colony rules, putting them all at risk of discovery by the unsuspecting earthlings, he knows his duty. What he should do is lock her in the brig. What he does do is ignore all the rules he's spent his career upholding.

Cam's also been burned by love before, but his mischievous Ria is a rule-breaker he can't resist.

Is she a heartbreaker, too?

MY BIG FAT ALIEN WEDDING
ALIENN, ARKANSAS 3

Lucinda Hayward Duvall, of the Designer-class Duvalls on Alpha-Prime, has never quite fit the mold in her noble family. Her four sisters are more beautiful, their behavior more acceptable and their bearing far more regal than she could ever pull off. Even so, she's happy enough with her books and her routines and to fall in line with the marriage arranged by her demanding parents. Until a chance encounter with a handsome stranger at a galactic way station on a wild and wonderful colony planet makes her question everything she's ever known.

Easygoing Axel Grey, second son and head of communications for the family business at the Big Bang Truck Stop in Alienn, Arkansas, doesn't care a lick of spit for protocol or pompous off-world VIPs. On the other hand, he has all the time in the world for a captivating young woman with red-streaked hair, a mesmerizing smile and a contagious sense of wonder. One stolen dance in a convenience store doorway later and he's ready to give Lucy anything…including his heart.

Lucy basks in Axel's admiration, blossoming under his regard like a flower starved of sunlight. In their too-short time together, he makes her feel amazing instead of awkward, a treasure instead of an obligation.

Of course, a future together is impossible. Her mother has seen to that.

AVAILABLE NOW

BIKER
BAD BOYS IN BIG TROUBLE 1

Despite the danger, there are some definite pluses to undercover agent Zak Langston's current alias as a mechanic slash low-life criminal. He doesn't have to shave regularly or keep his hair military short. He gets to ride a damn fine Harley. And then there's the sweet, sexy lady next door who likes to sneak peeks at his butt. Yeah, that was a major plus.

Kaitlin Price has had the worst luck with men. As if her unearned reputation as a frigid tease isn't enough, she also has to deal with her stepsister's casual cruelty and taunting tales of sexual conquests she can only dream of. So Kaitlin has never been with a man. So what? So what…

So maybe the sexy bad boy next door would be willing to help her with that.

Gunfire, gangsters and a kidnapping weren't part of her Deflower Kaitlin plan. Good thing for her bad boy Zak is very, very good. At everything.

BOUNCER
BAD BOYS IN BIG TROUBLE 2

DEA Agent Reece Langston has spent a year at the city's hottest club, working his way closer to the core of a money laundering operation. Women throw themselves at him all the time, but there's only one he's interested in catching. And she won't even tell him her name.

FBI Agent Jessica Hayes doesn't know much about the sexy stranger except that he's tall, dark and gorgeous. Best of all, he seems just as drawn to her as she is to him—in other words, he's the perfect man to show one kick-ass virgin what sex is all about. No names, no strings and no regrets.

Their one-night stand turns into two. Then a date. Then…maybe more.

Everything is going deliciously well until Jessica's boss orders her to use her lover to further an FBI operation.

Everything is going deliciously well until Reece's handler orders him to use his lover to get closer to his target.

Is their desire enough to match the danger and deception?

AVAILABLE NOW

BODYGUARD
BAD BOYS IN BIG TROUBLE 3

The baseball stadium is torture for Chloe Wakefield, from the noisy stands to the slimy man her colleague set her up with.

Too bad she isn't with the sexy stud seated on her other side. He shares his popcorn. Shields her from the crowd. And, when the kiss cam swings their way, gives her a lip-lock that knocks her socks into the next county.

Goodbye, vile blind date. Hello, gorgeous stranger.

Staying under the radar is pretty much a job requisite for bodyguard Deke Langston, but he can't resist tasting Chloe's sweet lips. Nor her sweet invitation into her bed, where the sensuous little virgin proceeds to blow his mind.

But someone doesn't like how close they are getting. The thought that scares Deke the most is that another woman in his care might be hurt because of his past.

All of Deke's skills are put to the test as he and Chloe race to solve the puzzle of who is plotting against them.

Chloe's in danger and Deke has never had a more precious body to guard.

AVAILABLE NOW

BOMB TECH
BAD BOYS IN BIG TROUBLE 4

Bomb tech and firefighter Alex Langston has a reputation around the station as a bad-boy, love 'em and leave 'em type, but that couldn't be further from the truth. He wants nothing more than a quiet life after a military tour that saw him in some very hot situations overseas. He garners more than his fair share of feminine attention, but hasn't felt so much as a spark of interest for any woman since landing in Ironwood, Arizona…until now.

Schoolteacher Veronica Quentin was warned to keep her guard up around Alex. The last thing she wants is to be a notch on some sexy stud's bedpost. She's been used before, and knows well the heartache that can bring. But that was before she saw him. And before he rescued her from a mysterious kidnapping that saw her chained half-naked in the town square with a bomb strapped to her chest.

But is Veronica the real target? Or has someone set their sights on Alex?

Until they find out, they can't trust anyone but each other. And the sensual flames that ignite whenever they're together.

AVAILABLE NOW

BOUNTY HUNTER
BAD BOYS IN BIG TROUBLE 5

Dalton Langston has a sixth sense when it comes to tracking his quarry. He has a talent for getting in his prey's mind. Now, the only thing he's interested in hunting is some rest and relaxation in Las Vegas. The last thing he wants is to get dragged into chasing after some runaway rich girl.

Lina Dragovic has eluded everyone her parents have sent after her in their efforts to force her into an arranged marriage. She's served her time as the Dragovic crime family's cloistered daughter. Now all she wants is her freedom. What better place to hide than Sin City, where the bright lights offer the deepest shadows?

But there's no outrunning the dangerously sexy bounty hunter...especially when getting caught by him is so tempting. And so deliciously rewarding.

Falling in love was never part of the plan.

BANDIT
BAD BOYS IN BIG TROUBLE 6

Miles Turner, a handler and operative with The Organization, a private security firm, is used to always being the man with the plan, the guy in control of everything around him. He can't imagine any situation that would get the better of him— until he meets Sophie.

Travelling sales rep Sophie Rayburn has been burned by love before, but she's determined not to spend Christmas Eve alone. When she spots sexy Miles at a run-down bar in a Podunk New Mexico bar, she decides he'd make the perfect gift to herself. Why shouldn't she indulge them both with a little holiday cheer between the sheets?

Sensual sparks fly as soon as they come together, like they were made for each other, in bed and out. A kidnapping, a drug scam and a dangerous mole don't stand a chance.

Sweet, sexy Sophie is enough to make even a good man lose total control. And Miles is not good. He's all bad boy.

COMING SOON

BILLIONAIRE
BAD BOYS IN BIG TROUBLE 7

About the Author

FIONA ROARKE is a multi-published author who lives a quiet life with the exception of the characters and stories roaming around in her head. She started writing about sexy alpha heroes, using them to launch her very first series, Bad Boys in Big Trouble. Her latest series is light, funny Sci-Fi contemporary romance set in Arkansas. When she's not curled on the sofa reading a great book or at the movie theater watching the latest action film, Fiona spends her time writing about the next bad boy (or bad boy alien) who needs his story told. Laughter is essential each and every day along with lots of coffee first thing in the morning.

Want to know when Fiona's next book will be available? Sign up for her Newsletter:
http://eepurl.com/bONukX

www.FionaRoarke.com
facebook.com/FionaRoarke
twitter.com/fiona_roarke